T. Russell Parker

T. Russell Parker

Capitol Street Academy

T. Russell Parker

ISBN: 979-8-83-290392-7

Dedication

To my mother Tammy, and my father, Terry.

Table of Contents

Prologue

Over seven hundred years ago, the world only knew war. Every kingdom sent their knights to battle, while every king and queen hoped for it all to end with their people coming out of it for the better. That wasn't the case however.

No matter how good their intentions of war were, every leader knew their conflicts caused their population to suffer. Parents cried when their sons left for the front lines, and they cried when they returned dead in the back of a horse carriage. The strife of wartime rushed the elderly who could move on their own to finish their daily routines, with many of them dying in the fields from heat strokes. The ones who couldn't make it under their own power were already dead. Mothers birthed children as fast as possible to replenish their dying populations, while the women too young or too old to bear children made materials for the knights.

Every leader wanted their war to end, but they knew if they stopped, the opposition would overrun them. They didn't trust the other nations to sort their differences through talking either. It seemed everything would come to an end one way or another, and so most nations figured they would go out fighting. With no other options but to fight, everyone turned to one queen.

She never had a name but because she had never fought a single battle, and war had never touched her kingdom, the expanding kingdoms had given her the title of The Peace Queen. The people who fled to her later discovered that magic protected her palace and its curtilage. This discovery came when King Edward of England journeyed to Peace Palace to find a solution to his country's war problems.

The Peace Queen listened to his concerns and decided to invite all the kings and queens of the known world to her palace to negotiate a way out of the darkness of war. She had her own proposal, and the only solution to world salvation—The Peace Treaty.

The magical contract ensured that so long as the signed name's bloodline continued to lead their nation, they could never start a war, and magic would always protect them. If a nation defies the treaty, their nation would instantly crumble.

Nearly everyone was on board with the Peace Treaty, but one man attempted to stop The Peace Queen. He battled her in the Chamber of Souls, but she defeated him. History knows him as The War King for his desire to continue all war and that he also possessed magic, much like The Peace Queen herself.

While it is unclear what happened after the Peace Treaty signing regarding The Peace Queen and The War King, the world flourished with prosperity and a new age of peacetime. For over seven hundred years, no one had battled each other. Instead, nations worked together to build a better future for their people. Technology advanced no longer for war purposes but for prolonging life.

One generation after the Peace Treaty signing, humanity developed its own magical powers in the form of three branches: physical, natural, and spiritual—each with their own unique abilities.

With science and magic combined, children of today were born into a world without war.

Chapter 1

Rebecca Warren never expected to be sitting in a closed-off section of an airport over three thousand miles from her home in Oxshott, England much less alone with her sister Isabelle. Their parents and the rest of their family were in hiding from the civil unrest in England. But here she was, reading a history book like it was a children's story to the girl with golden-blond hair mixed with a strand of pink-dyed hair and steel-blue eyes.

"I wish we could use magic," Isabelle said dreamily. "Wouldn't it be cool if they let us learn here?"

"I doubt it," Rebecca said. "We're still from England, and, if we return with those powers, they could be mean to us."

"The Peace Queen was a nice lady. I wish she could come back and tell England to let us learn and stop King Mathias."

As Isabelle said his name, Rebecca looked at a TV nearby and read the headline: King Mathias Calls for US to Cooperate on Handing Over Warren Sisters.

Two people appeared on-screen, talking to one another. The TV was muted, but, judging from their faces—which seemed tense and flustered—Rebecca knew they were debating if she and Isabelle belonged in America.

Their parents, Anthony and Valérie, had sent the girls to America. King Mathias Burgess had declared all wealthy and well-known people of England as enemies, and the Warrens were among that group of people.

Anthony was a worldwide soccer star who had made himself a household name. A few years ago, however, he suffered a career-ending injury that put him into a coaching career. Valérie used to work in the science field until very recently contracted a disease she was trying to find a way to prevent. She found success in her studies, but she would more than likely be the last person to die from the disease.

Both Rebecca and Isabelle's parents had plenty of money from their careers and had established a nice life for them, their older brother Ray, and their adopted sister Bianca. But Rebecca never cared for nice clothes, high-class parties, nor uppity schools with snobby people, like her previous school, Sixsprings Academy. All she ever wanted was to write, bake, and spend time with her father.

Anthony never made time for her though. He was never home enough to even speak to her. He was always away because of games, practices, training, public relations, and media stuff. Rebecca had hoped he would be around more when he got injured, but he had taken a coaching job in America, and it caused him to be gone for months at a time.

Rebecca had rebelled against him for it just so he would pay attention to her, but he never seemed to understand it. Luckily, Rebecca did have someone for a father figure—her godbrother Blake. He had never met his father, as he was murdered during his mother's pregnancy, so he understood Rebecca's situation. He and Isabelle were all Rebecca felt she had left. She knew her mother would likely be dead before she would get the chance to see her again; her brother was a fool, and her adopted sister was already grown and had moved on to do her own thing in archeology.

And now Isabelle was all she had left. Her father had sent them to America to seek refuge from King Mathias and tasked Rebecca with keeping Isabelle safe at all costs while their parents handled the situation back home.

Based on the airport TV's images, it did not seem like they were handling the situation at all. Buildings were on fire; people were running in fear of police with their swords and bows, and everything looked like total Hell.

"Rebecca and Isabelle Warren?"

Rebecca looked up. One of the airport security guards had approached them with a woman in sweat pants and a thermal shirt.

"What is it?" Rebecca asked.

"Your relative, Kate Warren, is here to collect you both."

"Hey there," the woman said with a friendly smile and wave. Kate was their second cousin. Their father was originally from America but had moved to England at a young age. Their mother was French.

"Hi, Kate!" Isabelle said, getting up to hug her. This was the first time they had ever met, and Isabelle was treating it like they've known each other forever. Rebecca, on the other hand, was perfectly fine with standing there watching it and not getting involved.

After Kate and Isabelle released and Rebecca made it clear she wouldn't do the same thing, the security guard escorted them from the lobby.

What waited for them on the other side of the doors was unnerving. The protesters who raged and yelled at the girls made them feel the chill of the fast-approaching fall weather of New York City. The signs the Americans held read, Get Out!, We Don't Want You!, and Go away! Rebecca was used to being unwanted, but she knew her sister perceived their situation differently.

Police had erected barricades to protect the girls' exit from attacking protestors, but Rebecca had to cover Isabelle's ears from the words they were shouting. It was amazing they somehow made it to Kate's car in one piece. While the king had outlawed magic in England, Americans could openly use theirs. She expected this place to be a wildland. Perhaps they were not far from it.

Kate's car had certainly seen better days. It was a beat-up red two-door sedan with front seats that folded forward to allow passengers to sit in the back. Despite it being a tight fit, even for Rebecca's medium size, she decided to sit in the back and let Isabelle have the front beside Kate. She didn't want to be the go-to person for a conversation.

While they chatted, Rebecca retrieved her journal and wrote in it. She had every thought that had ever crossed her mind in the book, and she had a lot to scribe at that moment, but Kate interrupted her.

"So that makes you sixteen then, Rebecca?"

"What?"

"Your age."

"Oh, yeah." Rebecca tried to sound as boring as possible to get Kate to leave her alone.

"I noticed you both have a similar hairstyle. I think the blue dye goes well with the black."

"Thanks. Isabelle did it."

"Yep! I was going to go with emerald green to match her eyes, but this azure color just fit her perfectly."

Rebecca returned to her journal, but she didn't get any more written, as they had arrived at Kate's apartment.

Rebecca and Isabelle followed Kate into the smallest living room and kitchen Rebecca had ever seen. The two rooms were not even separated. It was one, and the only difference was the change from tile to carpet. A hallway containing only three doors stopped short beside them. It was uncomfortable to even look at and to think this would be Rebecca's new home for the foreseeable future.

Kate noticed the look of disdain on Rebecca's face. "I know this is nothing compared to the mansion you guys are used to, but I hope this will be good enough."

"It's perfect!" Isabelle exclaimed. "I can eat breakfast and watch TV from the counter."

Rebecca faced Kate. "Will we be safe here?"

Kate hesitated then smiled. "Yes. You'll be safe. Nobody knows you're here."

"People were waiting for us at the airport," Rebecca reminded. "They know we're in America, and it won't take them long to notice that two new girls are in the neighborhood. Someone will recognize us."

"Well, you won't be here long anyway. Your new school is not even in New York." Kate unzipped her purse and removed a letter. "Capitol Street Academy in Washington, D.C. I guess your father paid for this one, because that's a big tuition fee, and that's quite a road trip we have on our hands."

"Capitol Street Academy?" Isabelle asked. "Isn't that the world-class public school?"

"No. It's a private school actually," Kate said.

"What's a private school?"

"A private school is the same thing as a public school, Issy, but they call it private here," Rebecca inputted.

"Wow. Things are a lot different here than back home. The cars drive on the other side of the road, and I saw a sign that said feet instead of meters."

"The people are not different though," Rebecca said to herself, remembering the protesters. Back home, people on the royal news called the Warren family a blight on the nation.

Rebecca turned her attention to the television. It was on the same channel as at the airport. They showed footage of the three of them leaving the place with all the protesters. And then his face appeared—brown hair and misty-blue eyes and a goatee and mustache. King Mathias stood in front of a podium and journalists.

One of them stood up to speak. "It is now confirmed that the Warren sisters are in America in the state of New York. What are your thoughts on this matter, and will you do anything to try to bring them back?"

Mathias was slow to speak, as always. It was like he didn't expect anyone to ask these types of questions, yet he always seemed to say the right things anyway.

"It is unfortunate that America and President Oppenheimer decided to negate our requests to surrender the Warren girls. I feel he does not trust me and my concern for the safety of not just my people, but his as well. You see, the Warrens are not just a threat to England, but now they will put the American people in danger by letting them walk freely. I will continue to speak with the president in a cooperative manner, for now, to attempt to retrieve them."

Another journalist spoke up. "Earlier today, you allowed Annabelle Alexandria to join your ranks in castle security just a week after setting her free from prison. Why is that?"

"First off, Annabelle was very wrongly accused of murder and kidnapping. As you all know, new evidence revealed she had nothing to do with the death of that poor boy. However, I need new members to my security team, given the state of things outside of this building. Annabelle is very skilled in combat and would suit the royal palace's needs well."

"If you guys are hungry, I have some frozen pizzas I can pop in the oven," Kate called out.

"Ooh, I love pizza!" Isabelle hopped off the kitchen stool and hurried to help.

"I'd rather lay down," Rebecca said. "Where's the bedroom?" Why she bothered to ask, she did not know, but it seemed obvious that one of the three doors would be her and her sister's room. Back home, the houses she went to were mansions and estates that resembled mazes if it was a first-time visit.

"You two are on the left," Kate answered.

Rebecca snatched up her bags and walked to her bedroom door. Quickly, she turned the knob, opened the door and closed it just as fast.

The room was so tiny that her and Isabelle's twin beds had to be stacked. Minimal walking space remained alongside a bedside table. The sliding closet door stretched one wall with an off-white color that hurt Rebecca's eyes. Their beds sat beneath the room's only window adorned with traditional blinds and above the same ugly carpet from the living room.

Rebecca knew she shouldn't complain about how aesthetically miserable the room looked. She could still be living in a basement somewhere in France near her annoying brother and father, and here, her sister was in less danger. On the other hand, she missed her mom and especially her godbrother.

Rebecca unzipped her luggage's front pocket and removed a photograph. In full vibrant color, she studied the numerous Warrens who filled the photo. Rebecca's gaze drifted to the left, where her godbrother stood. Blake Taylor was a tall man in his early twenties with curly brown hair and a face that never sprouted a single whisker. His blue eyes were from his mother, and everything else was inherited from his deceased father. Rebecca's dad had to be the father for Blake. She wondered sometimes if he was a better father to him than to her.

Rebecca regarded the girl beside Blake. The dark long-haired girl could have passed as Rebecca from behind, but the age and skin color difference gave it away.

Bianca was Rebecca's adopted sister but was the first child Rebecca's parents ever had. She was very good at school—another major difference as compared to Rebecca. Bianca had studied archaeology and had been very renowned for her work in the field.

Beside Bianca stood the best mother ever and to the right was the man Rebecca despised—her father. Just in front of them were Rebecca and Isabelle and beside them was Ray's black curly hair. He was always so enthralled in their father's soccer games that it was the only way they bonded, and Ray loved to rub it in Rebecca's face about how close they were.

Rebecca hated soccer ever since her first recreational game when she took a ball to the face, and everyone at school made jokes about it. She wished her father would have bonded with her much like he did with Ray.

Rebecca laid down on the lower bunk bed and stared at the picture for a while. She had no idea how long it would be until she saw any of them again. It seemed that King Mathias would continue to hunt down every Warren he could. Rebecca would give anything to take the fight to him. She begged her father to stay and fight, but he made her swear to protect Isabelle at all costs, not that she wouldn't anyway.

Rebecca almost didn't hear the bedroom door open as she poured her thoughts into the family photo. She tried to stash the picture under her pillow, thinking it was Isabelle. Instead, it was Kate who stood in the doorway.

"Pizza is ready, if you want some."

"I'm fine," Rebecca lied. She was hungry, but she didn't want to stop looking at the picture.

Kate did not leave the doorway like Rebecca expected. Instead, she entered and closed the door behind her then approached the bed and sat down. "What are you hiding?" She gestured at the pillow.

"Nothing."

Kate narrowed her eyes, and Rebecca removed the photo, knowing she wouldn't win this battle. She handed it to Kate, who examined it closely. Perhaps she couldn't recognize her cousin. Rebecca did not think she had seen him since he was a kid.

"How old is Bianca now?" Kate asked.

"Thirty-one."

"It was hard to believe when I found out your parents adopted someone at such a young age as they were, but given the circumstances, I guess they didn't have a choice."

"Was there something you wanted?" Rebecca asked in a harsh voice.

Kate handed back the photo. "I just wanted to chat. I know this is not the kind of living you're used to, and you'll be leaving for school in three days, but I just wanted to get to know you a bit. You're my cousin, and you'll be at my house after all."

Rebecca didn't know what to say about herself—or what to say at all. She expected Kate to scold her for not attending dinner.

"But it's completely fine if you want to ignore me," Kate noted. "I know you have a lot on your mind, but just know if you need someone to talk to, I'm here for you."

"I said I was fine."

"That was about the pizza." Kate smiled with uncertainty.

"And I'm fine with not talking. I really just want to be left alone." Kate sighed, stood from the bed and exited the room.

Rebecca was finally alone again. She returned to her photo but didn't want to look at it anymore, so she put it on the side table. She jotted her thoughts from the past few days into her journal, but, before she finished, the door opened again.

"I said I was fine, Kate!" Rebecca shouted. As she turned her head, her mouth gaped; it was Isabelle who stood frozen at the doorway with a slice of pizza in her hand.

"Oh, I'm sorry. I didn't mean—"

"What's wrong, Becky?" Isabelle asked.

Rebecca sighed. "Just … thinking about stuff."

Isabelle closed the door and yawned. "It's ten o'clock, so I figured I would go to bed now."

"Crap," Rebecca said. "I missed dinner, haven't I?" She knew it was her own fault, but time flew. The last time she peeked through the blinds, the sun was blinding her. Now it was completely dark. She hoped she would see stars, but too many streetlights sat at eye level to see.

Isabelle looked at the slice of pizza then at Rebecca. "You can have this one."

"No, that's yours. It's my fault I didn't eat."

"Seriously, I had too much already," Isabelle insisted. She brought over the food, and, before Rebecca could say no again, she caught the smell of its pepperonis enticing her. She took it without any hesitation.

"Thanks," Rebecca said, taking the slice and biting into it.

"Why were you shouting at Kate?"

Rebecca swallowed. "I was angry with her earlier. She wouldn't leave me alone."

"She's really nice. I think she wants to bond with us before we go to school. I noticed she doesn't have a lot of pictures on the walls. I think she's lonely."

"Maybe."

"What's this?" Isabelle picked up the photo Rebecca had laying on the bed table. "Did you take this from home?"

"Um, yeah. Just something I packed by accident." Rebecca felt hot in the face. She hoped her sister wouldn't burst into tears by looking at it.

"I really miss them. Do you think they're all right?"

"Of course. They're all looking out for each other. They're fine." Rebecca wasn't too confident in saying so, but she didn't want her sister to worry.

"Why do you think Mathias is really after us?" Isabelle asked, still staring at the picture.

"Dunno, but he's definitely a bad guy. We have to be careful and look out for each other."

"Yes, we do, but what about Kate?" Isabelle turned to look at the door.

"What about her?"

"Well, she's a Warren just like us. Is she in danger too?"

"I don't think many people know Kate's related to us. There are plenty of Warrens in the world. It's just we're famous, and Mathias wants the poor to screw over the wealthy just because we're rich."

"There's nothing wrong with people who are less fortunate."

"No, of course not. I just meant that he's probably leading them to believe we're the problem. Anyway, we should probably go to bed."

"Can you tell me a story first?"

"A story?" It amazed Rebecca that, despite being fifteen years old, Isabelle loved bedtime stories. She was still very much the same person as she was at eight years old—playful, innocent, and perhaps a little naive. She found everything either interesting or scary. Some might think her emotions were exaggerated, but Rebecca knew it was just the way she was, and, at times, it was refreshing to have that glow of hers around to remind her to not take life too seriously and just have fun with it.

"Sure," Rebecca said. She was happy to take her mind off everything in her life and jump into a storybook, even if it lasted for just a few minutes.

The girls sat beside each other after Isabelle selected a book from her luggage, and Rebecca read to her sister until she was fast asleep.

Chapter 2

The next two days were dull for Rebecca, as she had little motivation to get out and do anything interesting. She spent most of her time in her bedroom and only came out for food or to go to the bathroom. She took Isabelle's advice on being more friendly with Kate, but despite getting along with her cousin, Rebecca still did not feel like being around her.

It might have been because Kate would take every opportunity to talk to Rebecca about her interests and hobbies, but all Rebecca would say is she liked to write. When Kate asked her what she wrote about, Rebecca would just say it was private. It was the truth, because Rebecca kept her deepest feelings and secrets inside her journal. Not even Isabelle had permission to look inside it, because some of it directly pertained to her. Some of those had dated back years ago, but Rebecca had pressed those to the back of her mind, and she never wanted to think about it again.

The only other hobbies Rebecca had a knack for were listening to rock music and baking, which was her favorite thing to do with her mother. It wouldn't be the same if she did it with Kate though. The smell of fresh, warm bread just wouldn't hit Rebecca's nose as it would back home. Kate also had no rock music inside the apartment; however, she did find a Spice Girls CD.

But one morning, on the final day Rebecca and Isabelle had to stay with Kate, she awoke to the smell of cinnamon seeping through the ajar bedroom door. Rebecca assumed Isabelle had left it open. She checked the clock—8:00. It was an hour earlier than she had intended to get up, but the kitchen was calling her name, so she rose from the bed and headed for the door.

Rebecca's hearing senses overcame her smelling as pans and silverware clanged together with Kate and Isabelle laughing. Rebecca caught sight of them hanging out around the island counter, leaning into it and biting into crispy cinnamon rolls.

"Becky!" Isabelle exclaimed. "Come try one!"

Rebecca joined the girls. With her eyesight finally catching up to the rest of her senses, she saw the cinnamon rolls boasted a brilliant golden brown. She grabbed one and bit into it. If she wasn't wide awake before, she certainly was now.

"It's good," Rebecca said with a mouth full.

"Isabelle made them," Kate said. "She's a natural."

Rebecca finished her roll. "Well done, Issy."

"Thanks! But you know you're better at it than me."

Kate checked the clock on the microwave. "I suppose we should get ready for the journey."

The girls were traveling to school today, which was a few hundred miles and a five-hour drive away.

Rebecca chose her favorite green t-shirt to put over a black long sleeve, and she wore her classic black and white canvas shoes. She knew the style was abnormal for her high-class status, but she didn't care to dress up as her brother did. She wasn't into the Look at me, I'm rich! game.

The girls grabbed their luggage, which was hardly unpacked from when they had arrived, and followed Kate out of the apartment. Kate's car did not look like it could make the long trip. Rebecca wondered when the last time a mechanic had inspected it. She imagined the car being alive, and for every squeaky sound it made, it was a cry of pain.

Rebecca hated long trips too. They made her anxious about the destination, and the longer the trip, the more she worried. Attending this new school where people would surely know who she was made her think she would be alone. Sure, Isabelle would be there, but they were in different years. It was unlikely they would see each other much.

*****

After five hours of listening to pop music, looking at trees parallel to highways and feeling the rough ride of the car on the road, they finally arrived in Washington DC—a beautiful place adorned with Greek-like architecture. The streets were well kept, with trees and benches along the sidewalks. Some places had brick paths that led to the cathedral-like structures.

Rebecca noticed the ugly side of the city, however, where a large group of people stood out front of one building, holding signs that read, Deport The Warrens!

Rebecca wondered if they knew she and her sister were in the city. What if they were waiting for them at school? Would it be like the airport all over again?

They halted a few blocks down the road in front of a large fence with gold vertical bars. Three large gates of the same style sat in front of a white marble courtyard with a path leading to a neoclassical building. On the gates and fencing were three letters in a triangular formation inside of a circle that read, C-S-A.

Capitol Street Academy was not filled with protestors, but instead, many students and parents were gathered in the entrance courtyard unpacking their vehicles and traversing the main path.

Kate shifted the car into Park and flipped the trunk release while Isabelle let Rebecca out of the back seat with her luggage.

"Okay, girls, I guess we'll need to find out where your dorms are," Kate said as she unloaded Isabelle's luggage. "Let's go."

"Feels fantastic to get out of the car," Isabelle noted.

"It's a lot warmer here than back in New York," Rebecca said.

"Oh, Washington will still get its fair share of cold weather," Kate said. "I remember being here one time and got stuck at the airport because of the snow. The farther south you go, the more people act like it's a natural disaster. I just don't know how anyone in Hibernia can handle that heat though."

"You've been to Hibernia?" Isabelle asked curiously.

"Just to Carolina, but I saw enough to know that America should have never let them secede from the country. Their Confederate ways are awful."

As Isabelle and Kate discussed the politics of the southern nation, Rebecca found an information station and grabbed a brochure which contained a map of the school's main campus.

A girl standing nearby reading hers eyed Rebecca. "Are you a freshman too?" Her smile looked as though she had been practicing it all day and was waiting to make a new friend.

"Er. No. Transfer."

"That's still new like me, but you look familiar … Oh!" The girl regarded Rebecca with her mouth gaped and her eyes wide. She stared right at the strip of blue hair donning Rebecca.

The girl ran in another direction, and Rebecca rolled her eyes. If no one knew she was at this school, they would know soon enough.

"Where do we go?" Isabelle asked as she peered over Rebecca's shoulder at the map.

"Uh … Girls dormitories are this way." Rebecca pointed to a building marked west of the central building.

The main campus was just as stunning as the rest of DC. Nature proved just as prominent as the people, though Rebecca could have done without the people. A sign announced the species of trees that ran alongside the paths. Hackberries, sugar maples, and river birch were the most commonly present.

Once they found the girls dormitory, they stood in a line to get their room numbers and final registration papers, which came with stranger and more cautioned looks from the people nearby. Once they got through a rough security check, the girls could finally head to their rooms. Unfortunately, Rebecca and Isabelle had different rooms due to being in different classes. Isabelle, being a sophomore, had a room on the second floor, while Rebecca, as a junior, was on the third floor.

Kate decided to help Isabelle find her room, and that was okay with Rebecca. She stayed on the elevator as her sister and cousin exited onto the second floor. When Rebecca reached the third, she quickly rolled her luggage down the hallway. It seemed most everyone in her class had already arrived.

Girls congregated in front of their rooms, either socializing or hanging stuff on their doors. Punk rock blared from one room with a girl knocking hard, telling the resident to "Turn that crap off!"

Rebecca scanned the names on the doors to find her room. L. Shu and B. Lee, J. Maric and A. Black. Rebecca noticed one room had three girls assigned to it, whereas the rest had just two—V. Bancroft, S. Waldgrave, and C. Caspian. Rebecca recognized Bancroft's name from her old school's history class.

L. Ferguson was another familiar-sounding name, who was paired with R. Ward. Rebecca had a best friend, her only best friend, whose first initial was L and last name Ferguson. Perhaps it was just a coincidence, but Rebecca couldn't help but remember her old friend, Lucy. They weren't friends any longer though, because Rebecca had noticed last school year that Lucy was using her, and so Rebecca had cut her off, but she wasn't sure Lucy understood. She had kept trying to contact her during the summer. Rebecca would have responded, had it not been for all the drama with King Mathias.

Finally, Rebecca found her room—R. Warren and M. Wolfe. The door was already open, so Rebecca entered; however, her roommate was not inside, but her things were there. Rebecca put her journal on her bed and set her luggage beside it to survey her roommate's things. It was clear this girl loved horses, with all the pictures on her corkboard and a calendar. There was only one picture that Rebecca guessed could be her—a redhead on a black-and-white speckled steed.

"The rumours are true."

Rebecca jumped back to look at the doorframe. Three girls stood inside it, all glaring at her.

"Rebecca Warren is at my school," the one in the middle said. She had a brown ponytail that fell over her tanned shoulders. Rebecca thought the girl's face resembled the horses in the pictures.

"Can I help you?" Rebecca asked.

The three girls entered the room and spread out around her.

"You can start with telling me why you're here," horse-girl said.

"Because I go to school here." Rebecca knew that wasn't the answer the girl was hoping for.

The girl looked Rebecca up and down. "You know this school doesn't usually accept scum, so I want to know what made you the exception, considering you're a wanted criminal on the other side of the world."

"It's none of your business why I'm going to school here, so bugger off."

All three girls laughed at her.

"Bugger off? Is that your version of saying fuck off?"

Rebecca didn't respond.

"Let's start with introductions then, shall we?. I'm Vanessa Bancroft. I'm the most important person at this school, and you will listen to whatever I say. Capisce?"

"Funny. I don't see your name anywhere," Rebecca said, glancing around the room.

"My father is the reason this school still runs. He and the Saturn Society are the school's largest donors, therefore he owns this building and this room and, by default, so do I."

If what Vanessa said was true, Rebecca feared the repercussions of allowing this girl to provoke her. She didn't want to start any trouble at Capitol Street and be kicked out on day one, but Rebecca didn't think she would escape this situation so easily.

"Just get out of my room," Rebecca said with a bit of force behind it.

The girls laughed at her again.

"You still don't get it," Vanessa said, getting more serious. "I own this place. And let me tell you something. If your English ass tries anything, my father will personally put you on a plane back to your king himself."

Rebecca said nothing. She ignored Vanessa and unpacked her things.

This seemed to have disappointed the girls. Vanessa eyed Rebecca's bed and snatched her journal.

Rebecca made a dive to reach for it, but the other two girls stood between them.

That still didn't stop Rebecca from swinging. She shoved both girls out of the way and connected her right hand with Vanessa's left cheek. Rebecca didn't get much more though. Something hard and unseen hit her in the gut, and an invisible force threw her backward to the wall. She slid into a sitting position.

The two unnamed girls ran over, grabbed both of Rebecca's arms and held her down while Vanessa approached, holding her journal.

"I really miss home," Vanessa mocked as she read out loud. "I just wish my dad wasn't so famous, and maybe we wouldn't be in this mess. I hope Mum is doing well. I'm worried sick about her disease, and my sister might need help too. I just don't know what to do, but I want to fight." Vanessa flipped through the pages and regarded Rebecca with a grin.

Rebecca, however, fumed with anger.

Vanessa closed the journal and tossed it at her. "Daddy issues. Sick mom. Stupid sister. Pathetic. I guess you're just the angry person of the bunch."

"I'll kill you," Rebecca breathed.

"No, you won't. You'll probably off yourself before that happens, as depressing as your life is." She raised her hand toward Rebecca's roommate's desk. A pair of scissors flew to her, and she caught them. "Let's see. For hitting me, I think it's only fair I cut off that blue bit of your hair."

Vanessa charged Rebecca, who shook her head furiously, but the scissors never came close enough. A green rope-like thing snatched them from Vanessa's hand. Rebecca looked up to see a redheaded girl and a boy standing in the doorway.

"That's enough, Vanessa," the redhead said.

"Well, if it isn't morbid Morgan and her little native nerd," Vanessa taunted as she turned around.

"Get out of my room," Morgan said.

Rebecca noticed a plant on her desk that had extremely long vines growing out of it. The vines seemed to be moving by themselves and held the scissors, but Rebecca had a feeling Morgan had some kind of control over it.

Vanessa turned and beckoned for her friends to follow her. She called out over her shoulder, "I'll be seeing you around, Warren," and she and her friends were gone.

Morgan approached Rebecca, extending a hand to help her up. Rebecca took it and thanked her.

"What are roomies for?" Morgan asked with a peppy tone and a big smile on her pale white face.

Rebecca bent to collect her journal. She was so embarrassed that someone had dared to look in it. She thumbed through the pages as though she searched for where it was hurt the most, because, to her, anyone else's gaze on it were like knives digging into the journal's skin, and Vanessa's gaze was jagged and rough.

"Are you all right?" Morgan asked.

Rebecca noted the girl's ocean-blue eyes and closed the journal. "I'm fine. Thanks."

"Are you sure?" the boy asked. "You look like you got hit with something hard. Were you *pushed*?"

"Pushed?" Rebecca repeated.

"You know. Hit with magic?" Morgan clarified.

"No … or I don't think so. I've never really seen magic, at least not enough of it."

"How have you never seen magic?" Morgan asked.

"Well…" Rebecca wasn't sure if it was the best time to mention where she was from.

"Magic is outlawed in England, Morgan." the boy said. "It's the only country where it is completely outlawed and the only one that would punish a person who uses theirs by execution."

"Thanks, nerd." Morgan rolled her eyes.

"How did you know I'm from England?" Rebecca asked the boy.

"Apart from the accent, you're Rebecca Warren, judging by your hair."

Of course. How could Rebecca forget that she was famous? Well, notorious might be the proper term. People weren't lining up to get her autograph, like her father. They might as well be lining up to spit on her.

"Oh," Morgan said. "That makes sense now. I saw you on the news. Well, I'm sure everyone has. What's England like?"

"Er. Well, it's a terrible place to call home right now."

"Oh, I'm sorry," Morgan said. "Well, anyway. Since we know your name, we may as well tell you ours. I'm Morgan Wolfe, and this nerdy Tahoe is Andrew Lorette." Morgan leaned into Rebecca's ear and whispered very badly, "But I call him Andy, and he hates it."

"Yeah, I do," Andrew said as he pushed up his squared glasses. "Nice to meet you."

"We've been best friends since freshman year." Morgan leaned her elbow on Andrew's shoulder. "This poor boy was so shy that he'd get nervous being around his own shadow."

"And this girl was so bad in class that only the smartest kid in our year could save her."

"So, you're a Tahoe?" Rebecca asked, curious about his nationality. She had never met anyone outside of England, France, or America.

"Born in the Rockies. My ancestry is of about twelve different tribes. I was raised in the Eldorado forests and went to school in Sacramento."

"I've always heard Tahoes are still far behind in education," Rebecca said.

"Tahoma is full of smart people, and I have the grades to prove it. Our education system is statistically better than the civilized world, but America will never admit it. I came to the States because I wanted to get away from my family and see the world."

Rebecca scratched her ear. "Sorry, didn't mean to offend."

"Don't worry about it. I've heard way worse around here."

"I'm from Wisconsin," Morgan announced. "A farm town called Sheboygan. I miss my horses already, but they understand I'll be back."

"How do they understand?" Rebecca asked.

"I can talk to them, of course," Morgan said.

Rebecca cocked her head a bit.

"You really don't know anything about magic, do you?" Morgan asked again.

Rebecca shook her head.

"Well, get ready for it, because you'll see a lot of it here," Andrew said.

Chapter 3

Rebecca settled in with her new friends much faster than she had expected. Morgan didn't like the way her dresser sat between her bed and desk, so she and Rebecca rearranged them until the undecided redhead settled on what she liked. Andrew had left for his own dorm with the promise of seeing them again tomorrow in class. Morgan suggested they hook up her TV to watch a movie later. Kate and Isabelle stopped by to see how Rebecca was doing and to say that Kate was heading back for New York. When Kate left, Isabelle stuck around.

"Your plant is so cool," she said to Morgan.

"Wanna see a trick?"

Isabelle nodded, and Morgan waved her hand around the vines. They sprouted everywhere to form different shapes. One wrapped itself up Morgan's arm all the way to her neck. For a moment, Rebecca thought it would choke her. Before she could react, the vine stopped, and flowers popped out of it to make it look like a Hawaiian leis. Isabelle was amazed. "Can you teach me how to do that?"

"It's not exactly something you can learn very quickly. For one, it takes years to get a fully grown plant to work with you, and then you got to build trust with it."

"How does it trust you?"

"I've raised it since I was a kid. Fed it, watered it, all that jazz."

"I want to learn plant magic," Isabelle said. "Becky, can I?"

Rebecca wasn't sure what to say. She didn't quite grasp the whole idea of magic other than it existed.

Luckily, Morgan had an answer for Isabelle. "That may not be up to her or even you, given your circumstances."

"What if we did it in secret?" Isabelle asked.

"Absolutely not." Rebecca warned. "Issy, we can talk more about it later. It's ten o'clock, and you should probably get to bed."

"Um, about that." Isabelle fidgeted her thumbs as she stared at the ground.

"What is it?"

"Well … I don't know about sleeping without you around."

Morgan raised an eyebrow.

Rebecca knew exactly why she did but ignored it. "Look, I'm just upstairs if you need me. Think of it like I'm in the bunk bed, and I'm on the top bunk."

"Usually, I get the top bunk, but okay. I'll try to do it on my own this time."

She and Rebecca hugged and said goodnight.

When Isabelle left the room, Morgan turned to Rebecca. "She's like, fifteen and is scared to sleep alone?"

"You don't understand. She's … different."

"Clearly, but why's that?"

"She just is, okay?"

Morgan didn't ask another question, and, instead of pursuing the topic any further, she turned on the TV, and the two of them finished their night watching a crime drama.

*****

The next day, Rebecca awoke to a loud knock on their door. After adjusting her eyes to the early sunrise beaming through the cracks of the blinds, she looked at Morgan, who was fast asleep. Now knowing who should answer the door, Rebecca got up and headed over.

When she opened it, no one was there, but two long boxes labeled with Rebecca and Morgan's names sat on the floor. Rebecca gathered them and saw the Capitol Street Academy insignia on them with SCHEDULE & UNIFORMS listed as the contents.

Rebecca brought them in as Morgan stirred.

"Is tha … the schedule?" she asked with a yawn in the middle of her question.

"I think so." Rebecca handed Morgan her box before propping herself on her own bed to open hers. The schedule laid on top, and Rebecca unfolded it and read to herself.

Capitol Street Academy 2021-22 Academic Year Schedule
Issued to Rebecca Andrea Warren (11th grade)

Monday, Wednesday, Friday timetable:
10:00am-10:50am: Algebra II, Mr. Garter, Rollins Bld. 221
11:00am-11:50am: World History, Dr. Robertson, Bancroft Bld. 183
1:00pm-1:50pm: English III, Mr. Wallace, Caspian Bld. 104

Tuesday, Thursday timetable:
12:00pm-1:15pm: Biology, Mrs. Lambert, Waldgrave Bld. 117
2:00pm-3:15pm: Magiology, Miss Stetson, Bancroft Bld. 320
4:00pm-5:15pm: Culinary Arts, Mrs. Smith, Adler Bld. Kitchens

Official CSA clubs will begin recruiting during the first week of school. Students should contact the teacher or student leader in charge of their respective clubs. See your floor notice boards for more information on each club.

"Looks like I'll be learning magic after all," Rebecca said enthusiastically.

"You're in magiology too?" Morgan scanned her own schedule. Rebecca nodded, and Morgan smiled.

"That's at least one person I'll know in one of my classes. I bet we have all the basic classes together too. That's usually how roommates work. Can I see yours?"

Rebecca handed Morgan her schedule then inspected the uniform. The first thing she pulled from the box was a few pairs of black and white socks, which seemed knee or thigh high. Underneath them lay a couple of red plaid skirts Rebecca thought looked hideous, white button-up t-shirts—both long and short sleeves—with a red button-up vest and, finally, a navy-blue cardigan.

Rebecca surveyed her uniform with disgust. "Is this really what we have to wear?"

Morgan unfolded hers. "Yeah, I'm not a big fan of it either, but it's not that bad."

"I feel like I'm going to a brothel rather than class with this skirt! The ones we wore a Sixsprings were way more professional looking than this garbage. Can girls even wear pants?"

"Nope. I think the Saturn Society had them designed, but what can you do?" Morgan compared the two schedules. "Looks like we have just about everything together. You must not have decided on your concentration here."

"Right now, my concentration is on how pathetic this uniform is," Rebecca said, and Morgan laughed.

*****

It took some time, but Rebecca finally put on her uniform. She and Morgan stepped out the door and began their first week of classes.

Their first class was algebra II, a dull subject to Rebecca. She and Morgan found Andrew already at his desk with his textbook open to chapter twelve. The syllabus said they would start with chapter two. He wasn't the only familiar student in class either. Vanessa, Sheila, and Cassandra arrived just before the bell rang. They giggled at Rebecca as they took seats right behind her.

"She can't even pull off the uniform. How is she supposed to pull off a passing grade in here?" Vanessa said just loud enough for Rebecca to hear.

Rebecca turned to confront her, but the teacher, Mr. Garter, asked her to face the front. Just as she did, the classroom door opened and a tall, dark-haired boy entered. Rebecca couldn't help but look at him. The first thing that stood out were his blue eyes that sparkled like dazzling sapphires.

"Sorry I'm late, sir. I had an emergency with SGA."

"No worries, Mr. Parkton. Find a seat."

Rebecca thought he was about to sit beside her until Vanessa asked, "Join me, Alvie?" and he moved on.

In world history, Rebecca met one of the most interesting teachers she had ever encountered. Dr. Robertson was an old and burly man with a balding head and square-rimmed glasses. He was also not afraid to put Vanessa in her place when she spoke out of line, which was a relief to Rebecca.

"A few of you are new here." Dr. Robertson looked directly at Rebecca. "And while I do have a PhD, you may refer to me as Doctor, Professor, or even Mister. However, I prefer the title of Genius."

This got a few laughs from the class except for Vanessa who whispered something rude. Dr. Robertson must've had bat-like hearing, because he immediately docked five points off Vanessa's participation grade.

"And you can tell your father I did that," he noted.

Mr. Wallace in English III, however, was the complete opposite of Dr. Robertson. In fact, it seemed he feared Vanessa. His smile was so fake that it looked as though someone had glued it to stay put. When Rebecca entered the classroom, something caught her foot, and she fell face first to the floor.

"You bitch!" Morgan shouted.

Rebecca faced upward to see Vanessa sniggering. Furious, she stood and started toward her.

"Miss Warren," Mr. Wallace barked. "I suggest you go to your seat immediately."

"But sir," Morgan started, "Vanessa tripped her."

"You too, Miss Wolfe. I won't tolerate your nonsense and lies this year about Miss Bancroft."

The second day of classes wasn't all that much better, but it was certainly more interesting. Rebecca's first class was biology. As Rebecca entered, she couldn't believe her eyes when she saw a pale-skinned girl with brown shoulder-length hair sitting at a desk.

"Rebecca!" the girl cried out as she ran to her and wrapped Rebecca into a hug.

"Lucy? What are you doing here?"

"Well, I imagine for the same reasons you're here too."

Lucy was Rebecca's only friend back home. It was because of her that Rebecca could fend for herself from bullies, but, as time went on, Rebecca regarded Lucy as kind of a bully herself. She would always copy Rebecca's homework and never do anything for herself. It was like taking care of a younger sibling, but Rebecca had an easier time with Isabelle. It had been hard to break off their friendship when Rebecca did so last school year. The two hadn't been on speaking terms since.

"Is he after you too?" Rebecca asked in a low voice. She didn't like talking about Mathias in front of other people. It felt like they listened more intently when someone mentioned his name.

"I don't think he is, but Mum moved us here as a precaution. We should totally catch up after class. Apart from the whole king stuff, my summer was insane."

"Er, Luce?" Rebecca started, but the bell rang.

"Sit with me," Lucy said quickly and pulled Rebecca by the hand to sit down.

Rebecca looked back at Morgan and Andrew, both who were scrutinizing their interaction. They shrugged at her, and she felt she could do nothing but sit through it.

After class, Lucy invited Rebecca for lunch. She wasn't up for it, but every time she tried to decline, Lucy would mention something she had done over the summer break. It was as though Lucy knew Rebecca's intentions, but she was doing everything she could to avoid hearing what Rebecca had to say.

"Hey, Becca!" Morgan called out as she pulled Andrew along to catch up to them.

His free hand had been holding a notepad, and he wouldn't take his eyes off it until Morgan snatched him.

"Mrs. Lambert is pretty cool, huh?"

"Excuse you," Lucy butted in. "We're trying to catch up."

"No," Rebecca said. "Excuse you, Lucy, but you and I have been finished since last year. We are not catching up, and we are not friends anymore."

"B-b-but I thought we were past that?" Lucy's eyes watered.

"Just because we're in a new place doesn't mean we ever got past anything. And, by the looks of things, you haven't changed. You're trying to insult my new friends. I'm not sitting on the sidelines for that. Ugh, you made me say sidelines, like I'm my father."

Lucy gritted her teeth and balled her fists, then she stormed away from Rebecca.

Rebecca felt hot under the collar, so she loosened her tie and pulled up one of her stockings that was falling. "Stupid uniform," she muttered then faced Morgan and Andrew.

"Thanks," Morgan said.

"No. Thank you. I meant that, when I said you're my friends. You're the only two who have accepted me here."

"Of course, we are," Andrew said. "We're all in the same boat together."

"Except, not all of us are being chased down by a king, but, maybe one day, we'll get there," Morgan said with a wink.

Rebecca thought that was the end of crazy encounters for the day, but she was mistaken. One of her last classes of the day was the one she'd anticipated since she'd seen it—magiology.

"I was told this class was fun," Morgan said as they entered the classroom.

"Magic is a bit overrated," Andrew said.

"Says the guy who spends all day reading books," Morgan said.

"Also says the girl who has never opened a book for leisure."

"There's no such thing as reading for fun but being outdoors on horseback is."

Rebecca saw the back of her foe's head as she sat at a desk. "Is the teacher another one in Vanessa's pocket?"

"I don't know much about her," Andrew said. "This is the only subject she's involved with besides dueling club."

Rebecca noticed several awards sitting on a shelf. She went to read them. Each award was addressed to a Neveah Stetson, with all of them related to magic dueling or something called gladius. This teacher seemed to be the real deal. She had won in America, Hibernia, and Canada and had a recent world-class title.

"Will you sit down, so we can start class?"

Rebeca startled at the voice. She turned to see a tall woman with short jet-black hair and dressed in a black blazer and pencil skirt. Her eyes, as brown as an oak, stared coldly at Rebecca.

"Sorry. I was just looking."

"Apologies are worthless to me. Now sit."

Rebecca no longer cared about the awards or even if the teacher had saved someone's life. She immediately hated Miss Stetson's attitude.

Rebecca took her seat beside Andrew. Lucy was also in the class. Judging by the redness in her face, Rebecca assumed she had been crying, but she made no effort to look around her. Instead, she had her nose in her textbook. An unusual sight to see, had they been back at Sixsprings Academy back home.

The door shut, and Miss Stetson moved to the front of the class. All eyes trained on her, and no one made any noise other than the teacher's heels clicking across the hardwood floor. She stopped in front of her desk and surveyed the class.

"Welcome to magiology. Here you will learn the basics of what magic is and develop your cores. As you all should know, magic is the human being's second-best tool. The first one is the brain. So, if you can't use that, you will fail this class and probably at life itself." She panned the classroom for a moment before her gaze fell on Rebecca. "Miss Warren, come to the front."

All eyes fell on Rebecca. She hesitated to stand, but she didn't want to end up in any more trouble. She got out of her seat and approached Miss Stetson, who turned to grab a crowbar from her desk. Was this punishment for not sitting down? Getting beat with a piece of metal?

Miss Stetson stretched it out to hand it to Rebecca. "Bend this."

Rebecca was completely puzzled. While she was grateful she wasn't getting slapped around with the thing, she questioned how on Earth she would bend it.

"Go on then. We haven't got all day."

Rebecca grabbed the crowbar with both hands. She truly tried to bend the cold metal bar. She even gritted her teeth. She imagined it as being Vanessa's neck, which was more than enough encouragement, but nothing happened.

Stetson snatched the crowbar. "This is the result of someone who has never learned about magic. England is the only country to completely outlaw the practice. The use of it is punishable by death. During this week's lesson, we'll cover the history of how magic came about. But, for now, this is what you'll be looking forward to doing in the future."

Miss Stetson dropped the crowbar, and Rebecca and the class waited to hear it crash to the floor. Instead, it levitated just inches from the ground. Stetson outstretched her hand, and the bar rose to level with her chest. In a swift gesture, the crowbar bent and snapped in half like a toothpick. A round of applause erupted from some students.

Stetson eyed Rebecca. "And you're supposed to be his daughter?"

Neveah Stetson

Chapter 4

Throughout the class period and afterward, Rebecca pondered what Miss Stetson had said to her. What did she mean by, his daughter? Rebecca told Morgan and Andrew about it, and they both seemed to think it was about her father being a famous soccer player, but Rebecca felt it was more than that.

The thoughts left her mind, however, when Rebecca entered culinary arts. A familiar smell of baked bread wafted inside. This was perhaps the best welcome Rebecca received from all her classes. What made it better was Vanessa wasn't in this class. Unfortunately, Sheila and Cassandra were, but they didn't seem to care about Rebecca's presence. She assumed they only felt tough when Vanessa was around. Lucy was also in the class, but, as she had done in magiology, she was already reading her book and not paying attention to her surroundings. At least this time, she didn't seem to be upset.

But it wasn't any of those girls who had really caught Rebecca's attention. It was Alvin Parkton, the boy from her algebra class. Rebecca could not help that she was so easily drawn to him, but she still hadn't forgotten that he had chosen to sit with Vanessa.

Morgan cleared her throat. "Well, I think I'll sit with Regan Ward. I think you already have your partner figured out."

"Partner?" Rebecca asked.

"The syllabus said we have to have a partner." Morgan pointed to a piece of paper.

"Oh, well … I don't know."

"Go for it. It's not like you have nothing to lose by talking to him. And if he doesn't want to partner with you, there's always Alexis Black." Morgan pointed at a girl with rugged dirty-blond hair. She looked sickly, with puffy eyes and a couple Band-Aids on each arm, and her coughing sounded like a smoker's.

"Fine. I'll give Alvin a shot then."

Morgan grinned and wished her good luck before heading for her partner.

Rebecca watched Alvin struggle to remove a textbook from his massive book bag. She took a deep breath and approached him. "Er. Hello." Rebecca focused on the bag, as she was too nervous to look at him directly.

He, however, tried to make eye contact as he looked up with a big smile. "Hey there."

"That's quite a lot of books you've got."

"Yeah, well. I'm an honor student in charge of three clubs and the student government president. You should see my desk."

Rebecca gave a little, "Ha!" She felt so stupid standing there with nothing interesting to say.

"You must be Rebecca Warren. I haven't seen you before, except for on the news."

"Oh, yes I am. That's okay, right?"

"Okay?" Alvin laughed. "Of course. I don't judge people based on what everyone else says. I prefer to get to know people." He looked around, perhaps to make sure people weren't watching or listening.

Rebecca glanced over to see Sheila and Cassandra looking in their direction. They were probably spying on Alvin for Vanessa.

"Hey, do you want to be my partner?" Alvin asked. "I don't think my friend has this class, so I'm gonna need one."

"Yes! I mean … I'd be happy to." She scratched her right ear as she looked at Morgan.

Of course, she was watching, and she winked.

Rebecca took her seat, and class soon began.

Alvin was a lot more interesting than Rebecca initially thought. Aside from being student government president, he oversaw the film club, where he'd direct a movie chronicling the school year to be presented at the end. He also ran the photography club and was the managing editor of the school paper. Alvin was conflicted between being involved in the news or in government after school. He was the first junior elected as president and managing editor.

Rebecca thought Alvin was genuinely a good person, which was why she felt he didn't need to be in politics, but she admired his ambitions. She didn't speak too much about herself besides mentioning what England used to be like before the mess with Mathias.

The class flew by, and, when it finished, Rebecca felt like she had butchered everything. She approached Morgan after telling Alvin goodbye to explain how bad she had been around him.

"Really?" Morgan asked. "Because, from my point of view, you were in a completely different world. I know it's only been a few days since we've met, but you were not being the Rebecca I know."

Rebecca grinned at how ridiculous she had probably looked.

The next day, Rebecca, Morgan, and Andrew walked to English together. Rebecca and Morgan explained to Andrew what had happened, but he was annoyed at the mention of Alvin.

"He nearly shut down the chess club last year, you know," Andrew noted.

"But he didn't," Morgan said.

"That's because I chucked the rule book at him, and he had no choice but to keep it going. If a minimum of six people are the club, it must keep going, unless the overseeing teacher decides otherwise."

"And how many were in the club?" Morgan asked.

"Six."

"You see, Becca. It had been five until Andrew asked me to claim to be a member, and, in order to prove it, he had to teach me chess in a single night."

Rebecca laughed, but her enjoyment didn't last long, because she suddenly tripped. She caught herself this time from falling. She turned to see Vanessa leaning against the wall, grinning.

"Oops. Bitches be trippin'."

No teacher was there to stop her this time. Rebecca charged right for her. She drew back her fist, but she couldn't bring it forward to contact Vanessa's bony face. Instead, a force lifted Rebecca off the ground and sent her into the wall behind her.

Vanessa smirked as her friends laughed.

Rebecca had a difficult time getting up. Being jettisoned into a concrete wall felt like looking at Alvin; it took her breath away, only this time it hurt.

"What the hell, Vanessa?"

A girl with a black bob hurried toward Vanessa. "Do that again and I'll have no choice but to suspend you from dueling club."

"Hey, she came at me. I was just defending myself." Vanessa raised her hands, as if a cop had told her to do so.

"Regan," Morgan said, "Vanessa tripped Rebecca. You should kick her out for that."

"Yeah, go ahead, Ward. Kick me out for something I didn't do. Everyone here saw what the English girl did. I had a right to defend myself. And if you know what's good for your parents, you won't even try."

"Don't let me see you do it again," Regan warned.

The classroom door opened, and Mr. Wallace stepped out with his usual fake smile.

Vanessa stuck out her tongue at Rebecca before entering the classroom.

"Alright, kids. Let's learn something fun and exciting today, shall we? Peace be with! What are you doing on the floor, Miss Warren? Get up. We don't tolerate dirty uniforms. That'll be five taken from today's participation."

Andrew lent a hand to help her up.

Before following him into the classroom, Regan stopped them and Morgan. "Hey, if you want to get back at Vanessa, you should sign up for dueling club. Here's a flyer." Regan handed Rebecca a sheet of paper. The date for the first meeting was this upcoming Friday.

"Thanks," Rebecca said, studying the page with great interest.

*****

It was settled that they would attend the meeting. Andrew declined, since chess club met at the same time. Rebecca noticed Morgan seemed disappointed. Nevertheless, the girls headed for the dueling club meet, located at the indoor sports arena on the northwest side of campus.

One might expect to find a set of basketball hoops or a volleyball net in place. Instead, a half wall, kind of like in a hockey rink, formed along what would be the out-of-bounds line. Inside the walls were not hardwood floor, but sand, gravel, and a small pool of water filled the area, along with other various objects, such as pillows, chairs, a table, and even a car tire.

Alongside this area was another place that held swords and other sharp objects. On the other side were bows, crossbows, arrows, and targets.

Rebecca and Morgan both looked around, expecting someone to greet them, but the only people hanging around were Vanessa, Sheila, and Cassandra. Sheila sharpened an arrow while Cassandra suited up for what looked like a battle. Vanessa, on the other hand, sipped from a mug by a coffee pot. The mug read, Coffee is mightier than the sword.

"Well, look who it is, girls," she said, staring right at Rebecca. "I heard Regan asked them to come, but I didn't think they would."

"Hope you burn your taste buds," Morgan called out. "Oh wait, you don't have any taste … in being a decent human being."

"Girls!" Regan entered the room dressed in lightweight armor and carrying a sword on her shoulder. "Save it for the battles. Miss Stetson will be here shortly, as will the rest of the members. Now, Vanessa, do you have a full core yet?"

Vanessa raised her mug. "I'm working on it."

"Hurry it up," Regan said, "Morgan, what will you and Rebecca be interested in learning?"

"Well, I can't really participate in magic, since I'm a natural," Morgan said.

"A natural?" Rebecca asked.

"You can develop three types of magical cores," Regan said. "Physical, natural, and spiritual. Magic dueling is typically done with a physical core."

"I could easily whip everyone here with my vine, but I guess I'll do swordplay," Morgan said.

"It's called gladius dueling," Regan corrected her. She turned to Rebecca.

"What does Vanessa do?" Rebecca asked as she eyed the girl now stretching.

"She specializes in magic but also does gladius," Regan said.

"I want to do magic."

Morgan and Regan exchanged looks. Rebecca could tell they were both concerned with her decision. Rebecca had zero magical ability, but she badly wanted revenge.

Regan cleared her throat. "Look, I would love nothing more than to see Vanessa get knocked on her ass, but she's the top in magic, and it'll take a while before you're even good enough to be in a duel."

"So, then I'll beat her in swords," Rebecca said.

"Gladius," Regan said. "And good. But you still have to train before you can challenge her."

Regan led Rebecca and Morgan to the gladius area where Cassandra was just finishing her routine. She looked at Rebecca and Morgan with disgust and walked to another spot. Regan oversaw gladius, and she was exceptionally good at it from what she was showing off.

A few minutes later, the gym filled with many people hoping to be part of the club or they were returning from last year and picking up where they had left off. Alexis Black was already enrolled from last year, participating in gladius. Despite her roughness, she could gracefully swing a blade. To Rebecca's surprise, Lucy had attended as well. She seemed interested in gladius too, but, when she saw Rebecca, she headed toward archery.

Miss Stetson finally arrived, and those hoping to duel in magic could try out. When she saw Rebecca training in swords, she seemed agitated by her presence.

Rebecca and Morgan were paired together in their first lesson. It mostly covered how to hold a sword, intensive training, and adopting the mindset of a close-quarters fighter. Morgan seemed afraid she would chop off Rebecca's head, but when they learned a move, she seemed rather scared to come close to Rebecca, who swung her sword wildly.

"Stop!" Regan shouted and used her own magic to snatch Rebecca's sword from her grasp. "Morgan, go work with Cassandra. Becca, you and me."

Morgan looked relieved as she backed away.

"Sorry," Rebecca said to her and Regan.

"No, you're fine. But you need to work on your control."

After about three hours of training, Rebecca had mastered the basics of swordplay. She felt great about her new ability, but she wanted to really test it.

"Alright, everyone," Miss Stetson called to the crowd. "It's time for the open challenge. Anyone who wants to duel now, step forward with your challenge."

No one seemed to want to participate. Miss Stetson switched on a video board in the arena that listed the top ten in each group. Regan topped the gladius dueling with twelve victories and seven losses. As for magic, Vanessa clinched top spot with fifteen wins and two losses. Rebecca also noticed Vanessa was second in gladius with ten wins and five losses.

Rebecca stepped forward.

Vanessa tried to stifle laughter while numerous whispers scattered around the arena.

"Well, this is certainly a surprise, Miss Warren," Miss Stetson said, "but I don't think you are—"

"I challenge Vanessa Bancroft," Rebecca interrupted.

Vanessa lost it and busted out laughing. A few others joined in.

"Becca," Regan whispered. "Remember what I said earlier about magic dueling Vanessa? That also applies to gladius."

"I don't care how good she is. I want to fight her."

"I'll fight you, Warren," Vanessa said, "Cassandra, bring me my sword and shield."

Cassandra hurried to hand a blade with a golden hilt and a shield adorned with a black B to Vanessa, who was already suiting up her armor.

Rebecca gathered her own sword and shield and entered the battle box to await her opponent.

Classmates retrieved their cellphones left and right when Vanessa finally stepped in.

Rebecca suddenly felt nervous.

Regan stepped forward to ring a buzzer, and the fight began. The first to fall to both knees or their back would lose.

Rebecca charged at Vanessa but made no connection. Instead, Vanessa used her shield to trip Rebecca onto one knee. Rebecca raised her shield to block the onslaught of Vanessa's attacks. It proved too much for her, and a final blow of Vanessa's shield sent Rebecca flat on her back. It was over in a flash.

The crowd cheered as Vanessa stepped closer to Rebecca and whispered something about being a disappointment to her family.

"Back off!" someone shouted at her.

Rebecca thought it must have been Morgan. She tried to stand, but the armor felt a lot heavier than before. It was obvious that Rebecca needed to train harder going forward. Vanessa really was good.

Chapter 5

R ebecca's fight had become an overnight talk of the school, and it was embarrassing to say the least. She had no interest in getting out of bed. At least it was a Saturday, so she could stay in all she wanted without classes bothering her, but Rebecca had made a promise to Isabelle to hang out with her.

Rebecca and Morgan lay in their beds as Morgan flipped through the television channels, trying to find a nature show that usually started around noon.

"Oh, look," Morgan said as she stopped on a news channel showing a picture of the White House briefing room where it looked as though a press meeting had just wrapped up.

A news reporter appeared on the screen. "And you just watched the White House Chief of Staff address the media about the updates on the negotiations with England. It appears the president has not made any further progress on finding a solution with King Mathias on the English refugees in America. As it stands, the refugees will stay in America until England ends its civil unrest. Two major refugees are currently in hiding among Americans. Parliament considers Rebecca and Isabelle Warren, who are currently enrolled at Capitol Street Academy, extremely dangerous.

A video appeared on the screen of the same arena Rebecca had been in last night.

"A video leaked last night of one of the sisters participating in a fight with another girl. The brave student, identified as Vanessa Bancroft, swiftly stopped and disarmed Rebecca Warren. Bancroft is the daughter of Secretary of State, Victor Bancroft, who has been trying to persuade the president to extradite the Warrens to England."

"That is such horse crap," Morgan shouted. "First off, Vanessa is far from brave. Second, you aren't a threat; and thirdly, that fight was sanctioned. It wasn't like you tried to beat Vanessa to a pulp in the hallway."

"You think this is bad? You should've seen the propaganda Mathias had sold to the news channels back home," Rebecca said, now getting up to grab her things for a shower.

Morgan flipped off the TV. "Didn't you say Alvin was going into reporting or something?"

"He isn't sure if he wants to do that or be a politician."

"Both seem like corrupted jobs."

Rebecca laughed. She thought about the way England had treated them before they had to flee. When their favorite teen dramas would cut to commercial break, their names and pictures would appear on screen, and a voice would say things like, "This is the face of a bully. Report to an adult if you see these bad kids." Rebecca had stopped letting Isabelle watch TV and distracted her with outdoor activities—but never hide and seek, because, well, Rebecca didn't want to think about hide and seek.

"Well, I'm going to see my very dangerous sister, and we'll devise a plan to rule the world," Rebecca mocked.

"Oh no! I'm terrified!" Morgan waved her hands in the air like she was a hostage, and the girls laughed.

Rebecca left the dorm, headed down the hallway and found the showers. She didn't want to admit it to Morgan, but she was furious with the news report. Not about what they had said about Vanessa getting all the accolades, but the fact they had even found out and reported it. All it did was make things worse for her and Isabelle at Capitol Street. Sure, Rebecca didn't care about her own image, but she knew whatever she did also influenced how people regarded her sister. She hoped Isabelle had not seen the video, but Rebecca was sure it had gone viral. It must have, if the news got ahold of it.

As Rebecca showered, she realized the blue dye in her hair was fading. She would have to ask Isabelle to fix it for her, but maybe she shouldn't. People were starting to identify her with it, like that girl from the day they had moved in. Perhaps if she got rid of it, then nobody could point at her as the refugee.

After her shower and putting on clean clothes, Rebecca started down the hallway. She was in the middle of thinking about how she was grateful for not having to wear the school uniform on the weekends when she bumped into someone.

Alexis Black stood in front of her, looking at her flip phone— something Rebecca had thought no longer existed. Rebecca had a cellphone herself, but, when Mathias had acquired the throne, he had found a way to disconnect all the Warrens' phones.

"Hey, it's Alexis, right?" Rebecca asked as she approached her. "You okay?"

"Yeah ... No ... It's nothing. I'd rather not talk about it." Alexis continued walking without giving Rebecca a chance to speak.

Rebecca rolled her eyes. The one time she tried to be friendly to someone outside of her circle and it resulted in being blown off. Perhaps Alexis was one of those people afraid of Rebecca too.

She made her way down a floor and searched for Isabelle's dorm. Aside from Isabelle barging into Rebecca's dorm one night to sleep with her, neither of them had been able to see each other all week as they had been busy with classes. Seeing Isabelle would be refreshing for Rebecca after the week she'd had.

Rebecca found the door that read, F. PENDLETON & I. WARREN.

It had not occurred to Rebecca that Isabelle had a roommate too. She wondered how they got along. Rebecca knocked and waited.
A moment later, Isabelle burst out and wrapped her arms around Rebecca. "You're here! Come in and meet my new friend. You'll love her."

Isabelle pulled Rebecca inside, and a strawberry-blonde girl greeted her. She smiled at Rebecca with silvery-blue eyes.

"Becky, this is Faith Pendleton—my roommate and my new best friend."

"It's nice to meet you," Faith said. "Issy has told me a lot about you."

"I hope it was good things."

"Why would I tell her bad things?" Isabelle asked.

"Good point."

"You have a really cool sister," Faith said to Rebecca. "She's the best roommate I've ever had here."

"So, where are we going, Becky?" Isabelle asked. "I passed this water fountain on the way to art class, and it's really neat. We should go see it."

Faith smiled at Rebecca. It was the kind of smile that told someone they understood the situation of having someone like Isabelle around. Rebecca wondered if her sister had taken Faith to this very same water fountain, even though Rebecca was sure Faith had passed it numerous times before.

"Sure," Rebecca said. "I'll let you lead the way."

The two sisters were finally alone and could spend time together. Isabelle started talking about Faith, who was attending Capitol Street Academy on an art scholarship and a member of the dance club, which Isabelle had signed up for.

"And a boy in dance has offered to partner with me. He's really sweet."

"A boy?" Rebecca asked.

"Yeah. His name is Ryan Bostick, and he's in the same year as me and Faith."

"Well, just be careful with him. You know these uniforms aren't that great for us girls, and some guys probably enjoy them too much."

"Oh, he's not that kind of boy. He's just really nice and helpful. He knows how to dance quite well too."

"Still, just be careful, okay? So, how are your classes?"

"Besides AP art, I have Earth science, geometry, political studies— I don't really like that class—also English II and cosmetology, my second favorite class. Which just made me realize, you need more blue dye."

The girls left the dormitory, and Isabelle led them down a pathway.

"I don't know if I want it anymore," Rebecca said. "I feel like people know who I am because of it."

"But that's your identity. It was so people would know it's you. Why are you afraid of that?"

"Look around, Issy. People are scared of me."

"Is this about that video?"

"You saw that?" Rebecca asked as they rounded a corner.

"A group of girls were talking about it in the showers this morning. I asked Faith, and she found it, though I think she regretted looking it up."

The water fountain was now in sight, and the girls stopped and sat by it. It was quiet, apart from the water rushing. Nobody else was in the area, just trees and walkways as far as Rebecca could see.

"Why are you fighting people?" Isabelle asked.

"I joined the dueling club." Rebecca hadn't been planning to tell Isabelle about it, but she knew it would be impossible to hide it from her forever.

"But why? Fighting isn't fun. You could get hurt, or you could hurt someone else."

"I know, but it's the only way I can get back at this girl without getting into trouble."

"What girl? The one in the video? But she beat you." Isabelle stood and faced Rebecca. "There are better ways to get back at people. In fact, you shouldn't even seek revenge. Whatever that girl said, you should forget about it. Remember all the trouble you got into at Sixsprings?"

Rebecca sighed. She wondered how it was so easy for Isabelle to ignore her bullies. So many kids had picked on her back home, but she never seemed to have an issue with them. In fact, it was Rebecca who had a problem with them, and those bullies were the reason the teachers had sent Rebecca to the office and home multiple times. There was a time when Rebecca didn't stand up for herself though, and she had let people walk over her.

At one point, it had been Lucy who stood up for Rebecca and took the blame, but one day, Lucy had pushed Rebecca into a fight with a girl, and ever since then, Rebecca was known to not be messed with. Those thoughts ran through Rebecca's mind, and she started to miss having Lucy around.

"Promise me you'll stop the dueling."

Before Rebecca could answer, a familiar jet-black-haired boy entered her view.

Alvin Parkton looked at her, smiled and approached them. "Hey, Becca!"

"Hey, Alvin." Rebecca felt her cheeks go hot, and she had an urge to scratch her right ear.

Isabelle stepped aside to see who was joining them.

Rebecca stood quickly; although she instantly regretted it as her knees felt weak and wobbly.

"Whoa, are you all right?" Alvin asked as Rebecca nearly lost her balance.

"Yes. Totally fine. Er, how's it going?"

"Great! I'm just walking around, taking photos of the campus." He lifted a camera that hung around his neck.

"Cool. Did you catch anything yet? Or whatever the term is."

"Actually, I was over there, and I saw you and your friend sitting here, and I thought it was a really cool photo-op, so, if you don't mind, I'd like to use it for the yearbook." Alvin pressed buttons on his camera then turned it to show Rebecca and Isabelle.

It was Rebecca frozen at a point where she had her eyes closed. It looked as though she was thinking to herself, or she had earbuds on and was listening intently to music.

"That's really good!" Isabelle said excitedly.

"Yeah it is, but maybe next time you should ask before taking the photo?" Rebecca suggested.

"But then that would have ruined the moment. If I had asked you to pose, it would take away all of the emotion on your faces. Which, I must ask, is everything okay? You both looked like you were talking about something serious."

"It's nothing," Rebecca said.

"So, who are you, Alvin?" Isabelle asked.

"I am Rebecca's ... cooking partner."

"Really? I didn't know there was a cooking class here! I wish I had that." Isabelle looked extremely annoyed about this news. She turned to Rebecca. "You better teach me some stuff from there."

Rebecca laughed. "Of course."

Out of nowhere, an arrow stuck Alvin's leg, and he bellowed. He reached for it and fell to the ground.

Rebecca panicked and grabbed Isabelle, and they jumped into the water fountain. A few more arrows narrowly missed them as they took cover behind the fountain's wall.

Alvin screamed in pain from the other side.

"What's going on?" Isabelle cried out. "Becky, make it stop! Please!"

Alvin's shouting turned into sobs, and he went quiet. Rebecca peeked over the wall to see him still clenching his leg. She looked past him and watched a figure fleeing behind a group of trees. Rebecca leaped from the fountain, her clothes soaked with water, but Alvin's pants were soaked with blood, and something green oozed from the wound with the protruding arrow.

Isabelle shouted for help, but Rebecca thought someone would have come already after hearing Alvin's cries of pain.

He had passed out at this point—or maybe dead.

Rebecca wasn't sure if she could, but she tried to lift him. "Issy, can you help me?"

Isabelle hurried over, and the sight of the blood caused her to shriek.

"Issy, I know it scares you, but we have to try to save him." Rebecca knew the sight of something like this was nearly traumatizing for Isabelle. "Issy, listen to me. He'll be fine, but only if you help me get him to the right people."

"Can I just go find someone?"

"No. That person is still out there and could try to hurt you. You gotta stay with me and help me help him."

Isabelle was hyperventilating. Rebecca was afraid she would go into a panic attack. "Deep breaths, sis. It's okay. Everything is okay, but you must be strong and get through this. We can save him."

Isabelle's chest slowed. She swallowed hard and bent to grab Alvin's arm. The girls hoisted Alvin to his feet and struggled to get him moving. Somehow, they made it to where a crowd of students had gathered for some sort of event.

People screamed at the sight of Alvin. Two security officers hurried over and took Alvin into their care. A third, however, grabbed and handcuffed Rebecca and Isabelle.

"What are you doing?" Rebecca shouted.

"We were trying to help him!" Isabelle sobbed.

"Move it!" the officer said.

*****

Rebecca and Isabelle sat outside the infirmary about an hour later, still in wet clothing and their hands cuffed. The guards had given no reason to treat them like this, but Rebecca was sure they did it because of their last name. They had no idea what had happened to Alvin

A door clicked, and three people emerged from the room—a doctor, Dean Richardson, and Miss Stetson.

"You should know that Alvin will make a full recovery," Mr. Richardson said. "Doctor Muller here believes that without your aid, he would've lost his entire leg."

"The poison was made to subdue a human, but whoever concocted this one made it far too strong," Dr. Muller said. "I can only guess as to why someone would do such a thing, but I'm a doctor, not an investigator. I shall return to the room and let you two sort this out."

When Dr. Muller left them, Mr. Richardson spoke again. "My only question right now is, what happened? Neither of you have spoken a word about it."

"I'm not saying anything unless these cuffs get taken off me and my sister," Rebecca demanded.

"And why should we do that?" Miss Stetson asked.

"Because the only thing we did was save Alvin," Rebecca said.

Mr. Richardson pointed at the officer and ordered him to remove the handcuffs.

As soon as the girls were freed, they wrapped each other into a hug. Isabelle was still shaken from the incident and had not been properly comforted.

"Now, tell us what happened," Miss Stetson ordered.

Rebecca explained how Alvin had met them by the water fountain and that they were talking when someone attacked him. Rebecca also told them about the mysterious figure, which made Stetson's eyebrow raise. It seemed to be a shock to her more than it was for Richardson.

"This is truly disturbing," Mr. Richardson declared.

"Miss Warren, I'm curious," Stetson said. "If you didn't pull the string on this arrow, then who did?"

"I don't know who it was," Rebecca said.

"I happen to know my history on archery, and I recognized the markings on the arrowhead to be from England. And the wood from the shaft is of yew—the most common in Europe."

"I guess you'll just have to ask the attacker herself," Rebecca said.

"How do you know it was a her?"

"Just a wild guess."

They stared at each other for a moment, and Mr. Richardson cleared his throat. "Well, I suppose that's all the questions we have. You two can return to your dorms."

Rebecca and Isabelle excused themselves. As soon as they left the area, they ran into Vanessa, scrambling toward them.

"You bitch!" Vanessa spat. "You tried to kill him, didn't you? I swear, if he doesn't make it, I'll personally chop off your head and mail it to your king myself." She pushed Rebecca out of the way and disappeared out of sight.

Chapter 6

A few weeks had passed before Alvin was released from the infirmary. His absence from classes gave Rebecca time to ponder what had happened. She told Morgan and Andrew everything, from the attack to what Miss Stetson had said about the arrow. When they speculated on who might have attacked Rebecca and Isabelle, each had their own theories.

Morgan believed it was Stetson, who was really trying to throw Rebecca out of the school. "She's made it pretty clear that she hates you. If she knew your father before, maybe they had a bad run-in and she wants to use you to get back at him."

Andrew, on the other hand, thought it was someone from England working for Mathias. "With the arrow being from there and the poison meant to subdue, then perhaps someone was trying to kidnap all of you and take you back. And, if that's the case, then Mathias is breaking World Peace Laws."

Rebecca didn't care who it was; she just wanted the person dead and wished she could kill them herself. When she said this to her friends, they looked uncomfortable. The attacker had put Isabelle's life in danger, and Rebecca didn't want that to happen again. She had made a promise to her parents, to herself, that she would keep her sister safe.

Vanessa had her own twisted theory on what had happened to Alvin. She had started a rumor that Rebecca tried to sabotage Alvin's ability to run the student government; however, Rebecca learned that Vanessa was the vice president, so it would make more sense for her to try to take him out. Morgan and Andrew both believed she was trying to do that, but not in this situation.

"She only likes him so, when she wants something, he'll do it for her," Morgan said.

"She's manipulated him before in the past," Andrew noted. "I think it was her who tried to get him to shut down chess club. Now her sister is part of it."

"Vanessa has a sister?" Rebecca asked.

"She's a wannabe nerd. She thinks she's smart, but she's just good at trickery and not actually playing the game."

Vanessa's story about the attack had spread, and now people avoided Rebecca in the hallways more than ever, and when she had no partner in culinary arts, Alexis seemed hesitant to let her sit with her. Teachers kept a closer eye on Rebecca, as though she might explode and attack them all. Mr. Wallace had taken participation points from Rebecca just because she dropped her pencil. Most of September and October was dreadful to say the least.

And to make matters worse, Rebecca swore she saw five television vans parked in the visitor lot with someone holding a microphone and standing in front of a camera. That night on Morgan's TV, those same reporters had been warning how dangerous Rebecca was to the school just on her presence alone. Victor Bancroft had also appeared, arguing for the removal of the Warrens. Mr. Bancroft was the US Secretary of State, which meant he regularly dealt with foreign affairs. Mr. Bancroft was also the head of the Saturn Society, a political party very outspoken on keeping things the way they were. Rebecca posed a threat to American traditions, according to Mr. Bancroft.

Rebecca got to see Alvin again before algebra. He walked right by Vanessa as she tried to hug him.

"Hang on a second. I've got to see Rebecca," he said as he pushed on.

Vanessa looked as though steam was spewing from her ears.

Alvin stopped in front of Rebecca, Morgan, and Andrew.

"I wanted to say thanks for saving my leg. I literally wouldn't be standing here if it weren't for you and your sister."

"No problem," Rebecca said, trying to resist scratching her right ear for what seemed like the millionth time.

"Listen," Alvin said. "SGA is throwing a Halloween party next week at the rec center on campus, and I wanted to invite you."

"Oh," Rebecca said and looked at Morgan, who was grinning. Andrew shifted his weight back and forth and glanced at the floor.

"And your friends are welcome too. The more the merrier."

"Cool, I'll see what I have going on."

Alvin smiled and walked into class.

Fifty minutes later, Rebecca, Morgan, and Andrew exited the classroom.

"So, what are you two wearing to the party?" Morgan asked.

"Party?" Rebecca asked.

"The Halloween party Alvin invited you to, duh! You are going, right?"

"Doubt it. I hate parties."

She had dealt with enough of those from back home. Most of them were for high-class ballroom dancing. Just a bunch of snobby people pretending they were better than everyone else. Rebecca believed parties were for people who liked to boost their egos, and she had no doubt Vanessa would be there to try to outshine her.

"You mean to tell me that the boy of your dreams asked you out and you're not going?" Morgan asked.

"He's not the boy of my dreams. I mean, he's cute, but I'm not fawning over him."

"Oh yeah, so you just happen to sprout rose-colored cheeks from that white face of yours for no particular reason?" Morgan turned to Andrew. "Come on, help me out here. I know you saw her scratch her ear."

"I agree with Rebecca about not attending the party, but Morgan's right about your cheeks, and you do that ear thing a lot when you're nervous."

"Hold on. I refuse to go to this thing alone," Morgan said. "This party is usually difficult to get in to, if you don't know someone in the student government. Rebecca, you have my golden ticket."

"Fine. I'll go if Andrew goes."

Morgan batted her eyes at Andrew, who rolled his own. "I have studying to do that night."

"You study every night, you dork," Morgan teased. "Come on. Take a break and let loose for one night. You don't even have to dance, but you have to at least dress up. It is Halloween, after all."

*****

The day before the party, Morgan took them to a costume shop off campus. In order to go off campus, students had to sign out with a gatekeeper, and if a student didn't return by a certain time, they would face consequences. Students were also not allowed to go any farther than four blocks from campus, which was how far campus police patrolled. It was more freedom than Rebecca expected, even for her situation.

Morgan found exactly what she wanted to wear and held up it for all to see—a purple witch outfit. "Kind of ironic to dress up as what we already are."

"We're not witches," Andrew said. "Those who choose to do magic are called magicians. A witch is just a misunderstood spiritual magician, but folklore pegs them as crazy green women with warts."

Morgan rolled her eyes before they landed on an outfit.

"Ooh, Andy, this one's for you." She hurried to grab a white lab coat with crazy electric blue hair. "Mad scientist."

"Why not something like a vampire?" Andrew asked.

"Because everyone knows the two most overdone costumes are vampires and cats."

Andrew groaned.

"Now, Rebecca. Let's find you something cool."

It took them all day to search for something Rebecca liked. Zombie, dog, elf, supervillain—nothing seemed to speak to her.

"I think this elf one would suit Isabelle though," Rebecca mentioned as she took off the ears."

"You know what? I've got an idea." Morgan gathered black and white paint. "Do you have any dark clothes you don't mind getting messy?"

*****

On the following evening, just hours before heading to the party, Rebecca, Morgan, and Andrew were all in the girls' bedroom. Rebecca's eyes were closed as Morgan painted her face. She had no idea what it would look like. Morgan promised she would be a skeleton when she finished but having only Andrew's facial expressions to tell her how it looked didn't seem helpful. Morgan had painted bones on one of Rebecca's black t-shirts and dark jeans. Rebecca thought they looked moderately okay.

"Done!" Morgan chimed.

Rebecca opened her eyes.

Morgan stepped backward to admire her work, but she didn't seem as confident as she had been before.

Andrew scratched the back of his head.

"Is there a mirror in here?" Rebecca asked.

Morgan hesitantly grabbed one from her makeup bag and handed it over.

Rebecca couldn't recognize herself, and neither could she recognize a skeleton. Instead, a white blob stared back at her. All that was missing was two slices of kiwi on her eyes and she would be going to the party as a massage parlor client.

"Wh-what do you think?" Morgan trembled.

"Um …"

"I think art is not your forte," Andrew suggested.

"I'm so sorry, Becca. I just really thought this would be a cool thing to do."

"It's okay. I mean, it's terrible, yes, but it was fun."

"Terrible is an understatement," Andrew said.

"Shut up," Morgan said, "before I use my terrible art skills on you."

Everyone laughed and prepared to go to the Halloween party. It was a short distance from their dorm.

The party was already in full swing. The rec room was like a lounge, with seating along the walls. A punch bar was in the rear, which read NON-ALCOHOLIC above it, but Rebecca was certain that was a lie. The dance floor featured an orange light making everything look like an endless blinding sunset. The music was some trendy pop music, which sounded horrible to Rebecca. She preferred alternative rock, especially her favorite band, Pearlescent.

"Let's go for it!" Morgan said as she pulled Andrew toward the dance floor.

"I'm not, uh … ready. I'll get the drinks." He took his hand from Morgan's, who looked extremely disappointed, and headed in another direction.

"Becca?"

"I don't know how to dance to this kind of music, and it kinda sucks."

"Oh, come on. It's easy." Morgan took Rebecca's hand and pulled her into the middle of the dance floor.

Rebecca was more uncomfortable than ever before. She despised Morgan at this moment, but Morgan was having the time of her life. This was her element, but it wasn't for Rebecca. Not a minute longer, she hurried off the dance floor as Morgan dropped back into the crowd.

Rebecca went to find Andrew. She felt hot and sweaty, or was it someone else's sweat from when she had bumped into other people? She didn't want to think about it. She began to appreciate the ballroom dances she had attended back home. At least people had some respect for each other and gave everyone their space. This place was like animals stuffed inside a cage.

Rebecca searched the punch bar and could not find Andrew. She scanned the seating, with no sign of a mad scientist. Rebecca assumed he had ditched the party, and she contemplated doing the same, but she didn't want to upset Morgan; plus she thought it would be a good idea to ensure she didn't get into any trouble.

Rebecca found a table to sit at and watched the crowd dance. It was a disgusting sight, but she didn't have much else to do with her eyes. They had fallen on a vampire, and Rebecca recognized him instantly as Alvin. Three cats surrounded him, who Rebecca knew without a doubt was Vanessa, Cassandra, and Sheila. They were very interested in whatever Alvin was saying to them. It annoyed Rebecca how he even tolerated them. Alvin happened to look in Rebecca's direction. He stared for a second, perhaps trying to figure out who it was. He said something to Vanessa and walked in Rebecca's direction. She looked furious, and Rebecca's stomach dropped.

"Rebecca, is that you?" Alvin asked as he approached.

"Er, yeah. It is …" Now she had wished Morgan had applied the face paint correctly. Rebecca probably looked ridiculous to Alvin. She forced her right hand to grab the side of the table to stop it from reaching her ear.

"Nice skeleton. That's way more original and creative than anyone else here that I've seen. I think everyone else just bought their costumes. I know I'm guilty of it."

"Thanks. Nothing at the store really spoke to me," Rebecca said, feeling better about her appearance.

He sat next to her. "I just want to say thanks again for helping me with that attack. I really don't know if I could have kept attending school with a missing leg."

"Of course you could have. You just wouldn't have a leg up on the competition."

"Now, that's a terrible pun." Alvin laughed. "I may have to use that one for the school film. I'm nearly complete with the script. I've had a lot of time to work on it while in bed."

"That's cool." Rebecca's heart was pounding. She didn't know what to say to Alvin, and he seemed to be at a loss too.

His lips must have been glued, but he finally pulled them apart. "Hey, so I haven't had the chance to test my leg to make sure it still works properly with dancing, and I was wondering if you'd be interested in helping me with that?"

Rebecca smiled but looked down to hide it. Alvin had taken her by surprise with asking her to dance. "I don't know. This isn't really my style. Morgan already tried to pull me out there, and that's how I ended up here."

"What is your style? I'll get the DJ to play whatever you want. I'm the host of this party, after all." Alvin winked, which made Rebecca laugh.

"Well, that depends on what kind of dancing you want to do. Do you want to dance to ballroom or rock?"

"I've got an idea. Why don't we get warmed up with a bit of rock, then later we can slow it down with ballroom?"

"Will these people approve?" Rebecca asked, gesturing toward the crowd.

"I'm the student government president. What are they gonna do? Impeach me?"

Rebecca didn't understand what he meant, but she laughed anyway. Alvin went to find the DJ. A minute later, the music changed from pop to Evanescence, and Alvin returned to extend his hand to Rebecca, who took it without hesitation.

The two got on the dance floor. There weren't as many people as before, and now Rebecca was having a great time. It was perhaps the first time she could say she enjoyed being in America. The pounding of the drums, the rip on the guitar, and the voice of Amy Lee screamed into her mind, and she forgot everything around her and Alvin.

But that quickly changed when Vanessa approached them. "Hey, Alvie, why don't we go dance? I've got some important things to discuss with you about SGA."

"Um, I'm kind of busy." He flashed a nervous smirk and stammered. "Why don't we talk later or tomorrow?"

"Sorry, this can't wait." Vanessa took Alvin by the arm. "Come on, this will be fun."

Alvin had no choice, or at least that's how he made it out to be as he looked back at Rebecca over his shoulder.

Rebecca imagined shoving Vanessa's cat tail up something she wouldn't find comforting. Furious, she stormed after them, but she bumped into someone and knocked them over. It removed her attention from Alvin and Vanessa, and so she helped the person to their feet.

"Lucy?" Rebecca asked as she got a good look at the eyes under the mask.

"Rebecca!" Lucy shouted in happiness, but it seemed she realized they weren't friends still, because Lucy looked down and scrunched her nose. "Sorry," she said and kept moving.

Rebecca wanted to stop her, but she didn't know what to say or if she could say anything. She was worried about her former friend, but she remembered a promise she had made to herself after she had befriended Lucy, which was to leave people in the past. Still, it didn't help Rebecca from feeling sorry for Lucy.

She lost sight of Alvin and Vanessa. Rebecca had a feeling he was probably having more fun with her anyway, so she went to find Morgan. She was ready to leave this place.

It was quite easy to find Morgan though, because she was storming off the dance floor with people laughing at her with their phones out. Some event had completely redone Morgan's hair to look as though she had been electrocuted. She looked back to reveal her makeup to be pasty white with a red nose and lips. Her costume was ripped in different places too.

Capitol Street Academy

Chapter 7

As it turned out, Morgan was in the middle of a confrontation with Cassandra and Sheila when Cassandra had used her magic to attack Morgan. A drink had spilled and reacted with her hair and makeup, and her nose turned a shade of apple red. Morgan was certain it wasn't an actual drink. Andrew suggested it was some sort of chemical that had been snuck from a chemistry classroom. Rebecca questioned her friends why such a thing would be at a party.

"Some things make your magic work better or restores your core," Andrew explained. "Most people use coffee or chocolate, which work slow and harmless. But then you have harder drugs that can significantly restore your core and give a slight boost to your powers, but it's really disgusting, harmful, and illegal."

Morgan had freaked out about her new look though, because she had resembled a clown. Rebecca had the feeling that she was afraid of clowns, given that she didn't want to be around any mirrors.

The video of Morgan had appeared on everyone's social media. One had a caption that read, Morbid Morgan: The Class Clown. Morgan was on the heavier side but not overweight. She explained that Vanessa was the one who started the Morbid Morgan nickname, because she was overweight her freshman year, but it had been something she wanted to work on.

The name had stuck anyways, along with Andrew's Native Nerd. It was another one Vanessa had devised after he had beat her in a quiz game. Rebecca wondered if she would ever get a nickname with an alliteration.

But nicknames and Morgan's clown phase wasn't the most interesting topic Rebecca wanted to discuss. She had mentioned her encounter with Lucy to her friends, both of which wondered how she had been invited to the party.

"I bet she snuck in," Morgan said. "There's no way she knew anyone to get in. We wouldn't have gone if it weren't for your boyfriend needing his life saved."

"He's not my boyfriend," Rebecca corrected.

"Not yet," Morgan teased. "I saw ya'll dancing, and you said you didn't know how to dance. You got some smooth moves, and Alvin was falling all over it."

"Back to Lucy," Andrew interrupted. "Did she say anything to you?"

"She seemed happy to see me at first, but something seemed off about her. She wore a mask, but I could tell in her eyes she had some really deep thoughts going through her head."

"Do you think she feels guilty?" Morgan asked.

"Maybe," Rebecca said. "But that's just not her. She's never had regrets."

"People change," Andrew said. "Maybe she realizes what she did to you was wrong."

"Or maybe she feels guilty about something else," Morgan said. Rebecca and Andrew both looked at her.

"What if she tried to attack Rebecca and Isabelle?"

"Lucy attack me?" Rebecca asked. "No way."

"Well, the arrow that got stuck in Alvin's leg was from England. The only three people we know from England are at Capitol Street, and we know two of the three were the ones attacked, so what was the third one doing at that time?"

There was silence for a moment as everyone processed what Morgan had said. True, nobody knew where Lucy had been during the attack. The evidence pointed at someone from Rebecca's homeland.

"And besides Stetson and Vanessa, she's the only person I've had any conflict with here. And those two have made it obvious they don't like me. It's too easy to be them."

"I think there's a saying that it's those who are close to you that you have to watch out for more than your enemies, or something like that," Morgan said.

"Have you two forgotten Rebecca is in America for a reason?" Andrew asked.

"Because a maniac is sitting on the throne and wants me captured and killed," Rebecca said.

"Exactly. So, it makes more sense that Mathias sent someone here to capture you. Isn't Lucy also on the run?"

"She told me she didn't think Mathias was after her, but her mother brought them here just to be safe."

"She could have made that up," Morgan said. "Maybe she's here on Mathias' orders and is trying to rekindle their friendship so Rebecca doesn't see it coming."

Rebecca's head hurt. She was tired of listening to Morgan and Andrew discuss her problems. She didn't think it was Lucy trying to kill or capture her. They had been through too much for that to be the case. Even if Rebecca had completely shredded their friendship, Lucy was the only person to stand by her prior to the end of it.

"Guys, can we call it a night?" Rebecca asked as she sat up from her bed. "I'd like to go to bed early, so I can have plenty of energy for gladius training tomorrow."

"Sure, I'll head out," Andrew said. "I need to do some studying anyway."

"No, you don't," Morgan said. "If anything, books should be studying you."

Andrew grinned, said goodbye and exited the girls' dorm.

*****

Rebecca certainly had a long day of classes, but when they finished, she and Morgan walked together, with Andrew catching up to them.

"Off to dueling club then?" he asked.

"Yep," Morgan said. "You should come watch us."

"Can't. I have chess club. Big game today."

They rounded a corner, and two girls were looking at their phones. They glanced up and pointed at Morgan and giggled, then they hurried off when Morgan eyed them.

"You have got to ignore those people," Andrew said.

"Hey, Andrew!" a girl shouted from down the hallway.

At first, Rebecca thought it was Vanessa, but the girl was shorter.

"What do you want, Eva?" Andrew sneered.

"Good luck in your match today. After the beatdown I gave you last week, I don't think you'll be quite up to par anymore. How soaked were your pillows from all of that crying I caused you?"

Andrew didn't respond. Instead, Morgan spoke up. "You know, Andy might be too nice to say it, but you should consider fucking off right now before things get ugly for you and your stupid horse face."

"You're the one to talk about ugly faces." Eva laughed, turned on her heels and walked away.

"Who was that?" Rebecca asked.

"I'm so going to get her back!" Andrew snapped.

"What did she do?"

80

"I don't care if it's the last game I ever play, she's going down!" Andrew gritted his teeth and clenched his fists.

"Andy, calm down," Morgan said. "It's just a game of chess."

"No, it's not! I lost to her last week, and now I'm not the club vice president or the champion or anything."

Of all the things, Rebecca couldn't believe how passionate Andrew was for chess. She thought he had got into a fight, or maybe it was a quiz she beat him in; although that still would have been too much for all the emotion between them.

"So, who is she?" Rebecca asked again.

"Eva Bancroft," Andrew huffed. "Vanessa's younger sister."

"She's just as much of a nerd as Andrew is," Morgan added.

"No, she's nowhere near my intellect," Andrew said. "She distracted me in the last game, and it messed up my concentration. It won't happen again though, I promise you that."

Rebecca and Morgan finally left Andrew once he calmed down and was okay to attend chess club. Rebecca expressed her concerns about Andrew, but Morgan assured her that this was almost normal for him when it came to chess club or quizzes.

"The last time he got a B on a test, I didn't see him for an entire week outside of classes," Morgan said as they entered the arena. "I don't think he ever came out of his dorm unless it was to use the bathroom or eat, and I bet he still carried his books with him there too."

"Girls!" Regan shouted as they entered the gym. "Late! I don't understand. I have prepared everything for you two, and you've wasted ten minutes gossiping or whatever. Get suited up now!"

Rebecca and Morgan both rolled their eyes. Regan was obsessed with dueling, almost like Andrew was with chess. Tonight was a special meeting, because it marked the start of a short tournament. For this session, they would be qualifying to be placed into classes.

Cassandra was already dueling with another student. She was struggling against him, but she ended up taking him to his knees, and, for no apparent reason, she kicked him to be placed on his back, even though the fight was over.

"Cass, that was unnecessary!" Regan yelled, but Cassandra just shrugged her shoulders. "Alright, Rebecca, Morgan. You two are next. Don't hold back on each other, or I'll sit you both out."

Rebecca and Morgan entered the box, and their fight began. Rebecca had come a long way in her gladius dueling. Unfortunately, Morgan had not been as successful, and Rebecca made quick work on her.

"I suppose weight plays a big role in someone's performance," Vanessa called out from the sidelines.

"Do you want to test that theory?" Rebecca asked. "You can face me, and, when I beat you, it'll just prove I'm the best."

Vanessa laughed. "We've already done that. But how about this? Why don't Miss Morbid face off against Cass? If she wins, then your point is proven."

"Wait, Ness," Cassandra started, but Vanessa threw up her hand to silence her.

"I accept," Morgan said as she cracked her knuckles.

"Now hold on," Regan interrupted, getting in the middle of the four girls. "We still have to get through qualifying. We can do this during the open challenge."

"Isn't me and Cassandra next to fight anyway?" Morgan asked.

Regan scanned her clipboard. "No. I still need to get through two more matches."

"Well, I'm already in the box, so let's do it now."

Nobody waited for Regan to say anything. Vanessa pushed Cassandra into the box while Rebecca fist bumped Morgan. The two girls squared off, ready to go. Regan sighed and mumbled something about egos, but she went ahead and gave the signal to fight.

Cassandra swung at Morgan, and their swords collided; however, Morgan's broke at the hilt after the impact.

"Cassandra wins," Regan said dully. "Okay, let's move—"

"Wait a minute," Rebecca said. "Morgan deserves another shot, since her sword broke."

"Fine. Get a new one, and let's finish this up."

Morgan grabbed another sword and prepared for round two. The fight began again; however, Rebecca didn't watch the girls fight. Instead, she focused on Vanessa, who seemed to be concentrating way too hard on the fight.

Morgan's sword broke again. Vanessa's face relaxed, and she grinned at Rebecca.

"Cass, you've got a lot of power behind your swings," Regan noted. "But still a win. Sorry, Morgan."

"Wait."

"No, Becca. The rules clearly state that if—"

"One more time, but first, Vanessa has to turn around during the fight."

Regan tilted her head. Vanessa was taken aback by the stipulation.

"Fine, but this is the last time," Regan said, intrigued by this new rule.

Morgan grabbed another sword and returned to the box.

Vanessa groaned, but she did as she was supposed to. Rebecca stood face to face with the girl. They locked eyes the entire battle. This fight seemed to last a lot longer. Vanessa didn't seem happy at all either.

"Winner is Morgan!" Regan said.

Vanessa sighed heavily as Morgan cheered, and Cassandra whimpered. It seemed Morgan had dominated Cassandra the whole battle.

"You used your magic to snap Morgan's swords, didn't you?" Rebecca asked Vanessa.

"You can't prove it."

"No, she can't," Regan said.

Vanessa smiled and started to walk away.

"But I can still demote you on gladius, and I'll be informing Miss Stetson of what happened. She may also demote you in magic too."

Vanessa turned and her face went pink. "If you do that, I swear I'll make sure you lose your club president title, and my father will have your parents lose their jobs at the hospital. You know the Saturn Society funds that place and can easily take away enough money to get them fired."

"My parents are good enough to find other jobs anyway. Your father doesn't scare my family."

"We'll see about that," Vanessa said and she hurried away as Cassandra scampered from the battle box after her.

After the club meeting, Rebecca and Morgan chose to stay behind to help Regan put away equipment. They felt bad for her being dragged into their drama, but Regan noted that she was used to Vanessa's threats, even though she had never actually done anything.

Regan thanked them for their help, but she had plans to clean the floors too, so Rebecca and Morgan left. They laughed about how Vanessa had got caught cheating and how Cassandra was embarrassed. It all felt like everything was going in their favor.

The girls traversed the walking path. The night sky was pitch black with half a moon to barely light the way. Rebecca was distracted looking at the stars. It had been one of her favorite pastimes back home. She and her godbrother, Blake, had spent many nights together on the Warren Estate's rooftops. They had seen shooting stars, constellations, galaxies, and a plethora of interesting objects. Blake had a fascination for star travel. He wanted to be an engineer to hopefully be part of a mission to Mars. It seemed it could be possible with the use of magic, but Blake, like Rebecca, was prohibited to learn magic, with being an English citizen.

Suddenly, a hand covered Rebecca's mouth and another grabbed her arm. Morgan hadn't realized someone was attacking her friend, as she was a few steps ahead. Rebecca had to get her attention, so she did the only thing she could—she bit the hand that covered her mouth.

The woman bellowed.

Morgan looked back. The color in her face drained, but she hurried to Rebecca, lifted her hands outward then clapped them together. The trees nearby swung their branches wildly. One of them whipped Rebecca's face, and another hit the woman from behind, causing her to release Rebecca. The woman fled as Morgan waved her hands, trying to move more branches in an unnatural manner. The woman dodged each of them and escaped.

"Help!" Morgan screamed repeatedly.

A moment later, lights in a nearby dorm clicked on. Rebecca jumped up to chase after the woman, but the branches blocked her path, and Morgan grabbed her.

"No! She could be leading you into a trap."

"I'll kill you if you come back!" Rebecca screamed at the trees.

It didn't take long for someone to arrive to see what the commotion was. At least a dozen people appeared in their bedclothes and two security guards who asked what had happened.

"We were attacked by—"

"A dog," Rebecca finished. "A big one." She regarded Morgan, hoping she would go along.

"Yes, a ferocious dog is running loose, and it followed us as we left the arena. We fought it off, but we weren't sure it would give up."

The guards ordered everyone, including Rebecca and Morgan, to their dorms while they searched for the non-existent dog. When they arrived back, Morgan shut her door and asked Rebecca why she didn't want to tell the truth.

"Because nobody would believe us," she replied as she rubbed the spot where the branch had hit her. "They already think I'm behind Alvin's attack in some way. If they get wind of someone attacking me again, they'll use that as an excuse to expel me. And as much as I hate this school, I need to stay for Isabelle."

Then it hit Rebecca. She needed to check on her sister immediately. Without warning, she headed out the dorm room, bolted down the hallway and descended one flight. Rebecca found Isabelle and Faith's room and knocked hard.

A yawning Faith opened the door. "Can I haaalp you?"

"Is Isabelle inside?" Rebecca asked breathlessly.

"She's asleep. Well, maybe not after your knocking. Is everything okay?"

Rebecca sighed. "Yes, everything is all right. Just— can you have Isabelle meet me at my room in the morning? Actually, I'll just come down here and wait for her instead, but would you tell her not to leave the room without me being here?"

"Of course," Faith said, clearly confused with a puzzled look.

Rebecca said thanks and goodnight and headed back upstairs.

Chapter 8

Rebecca and Morgan explained to Andrew what had happened the next day at lunch in the cafeteria. His first question was why Rebecca didn't report it to the authorities. Rebecca told him she didn't think it would help anything but rather make things worse. One thing was for certain in her eyes; Lucy wasn't the attacker.

"No way Lucy has learned combat in such a short amount of time."

"But you have gotten really good yourself," Morgan noted. "You said you had not seen her since your last school year back home. That's been, like, six months, and you've been training here for just a few."

"There's just no way. She's only just started with archery and never does anything with close quarters. I won't believe it until I see it for myself. Until then, I think it was Vanessa or Stetson."

"I don't think so," Andrew said. "Did this woman use magic on you?"

"No. That was all Morgan's doing, which was really good, by the way."

Morgan beamed.

"Then it can't be either. They could have taken you easily if that was one of them, because they are both good at magic."

"Exactly," Morgan said. "So then that just leaves Lucy."

"Or someone from England," Andrew said.

"She still fits that description."

"It's not her!" Rebecca demanded. She felt flustered and was tired of all the blame they put on Lucy. She knew it wasn't her, and she wished her friends understood that. The two of them had been through so much together that they wouldn't betray each other like that. They had always been straight with each other from the beginning. Nothing had changed between them other than not being friends, which was the result of Lucy not changing to begin with.

Rebecca glanced at the clock. "I've gotta go. Isabelle is about to get out of class." She stood to pack her books.

"Are you still walking her to class?" Andrew asked.

"Yes, and I will keep doing it until the person attacking us is either captured or dead."

Rebecca said goodbye and headed out of the cafeteria. Ever since the attack, Rebecca had ensured that she escorted Isabelle to her classes. It caused Rebecca to be late for her own, but she didn't care. She had a feeling that if the attacker was someone the Bancrofts or Mathias had hired, they would try for Isabelle next. Rebecca would not let that happen.

She hadn't told Isabelle about what had happened. It would have only made things more terrifying for her, and Rebecca wanted her to feel safe. When Isabelle asked Rebecca about their new routine, Rebecca said she wanted to see her sister more, and Rebecca discussed all the new cooking recipes, which made Isabelle's day. She noted that they would have to try a few when they returned to Kate's apartment for winter break.

Rebecca headed to collect Isabelle from AP art to take her to dance club. Isabelle had become the top art student, and it looked as though she would be accelerated to honors class if she stayed next year. Rebecca was proud of her sister's accomplishments. It was always a relief for her to hear Isabelle discuss the things she did, except when she would mention Ryan Bostick—her friend who wanted more than friendship. Rebecca didn't particularly like him. He seemed way too nice, with the way Isabelle talked about him, but Rebecca had yet to meet him.

Rebecca stood outside the art classroom as the bell rang, and the students poured into the hallway.

"Miss Warren, Mr. Hill, and Miss Pendleton," the teacher called out. "You three will work together on the next group project. Yes, Jonas. You'll have to work with others."

A boy groaned as he exited the classroom. He nearly bumped into Rebecca as he mumbled something in what Rebecca thought was German. Isabelle and Faith followed from behind.

"I'm so excited," Isabelle said to her. "I know Jonas has a dark outlook on art, but it is really amazing what he can do. Maybe we can do a combination of life and death. Oh, hi, sis!"

Isabelle hugged Rebecca. People turned to keep from laughing. Rebecca wondered if Isabelle was dealing with any bullies. She shot each of them a look as they passed, and they all seemed to straighten up.

"Look what I'm doing!" Isabelle pulled a pencil drawing of what looked like a family portrait from her backpack.

Rebecca examined it. Isabelle was trying to mimic the family photo they had when they first arrived in America. Rebecca noticed a few different things. Everyone, including Rebecca, was smiling, and they all seemed happy. Rebecca held Blake in a tight hug, and Bianca was crouched down with her arms around Isabelle and Ray. In the middle, their parents hugged each other.

"This is brilliant, Issy."

"Thanks! I'm coloring it next, and hopefully Mrs. Galloway will let me print some to give to everyone."

Faith joined Rebecca and Isabelle on their journey to dance club since she was part of it too. Rebecca had come to like Faith a lot. She could see why Isabelle enjoyed her company. She was a good friend for Isabelle, the kind to be there when a sister couldn't. Faith had even let Isabelle dye a strip of her hair pink, which almost made them look like twins.

Faith was from Middletown, Connecticut. Her mother was a dentist, and her father worked in graphics design for World Dueling Entertainment—a scripted magic dueling sports league. Faith had explained that dueling was mostly illegal in America unless some members of the government approved it. As it turned out, illegal dueling was very popular anyway, especially in rural areas, so it never stopped anything.

The girls arrived at the dance hall. Rebecca usually left Isabelle at the classroom door and hurried to her own, but since she had nowhere to go, she decided to enter.

"Ryan!" Isabelle called out to a tall, blond-haired boy.
He grinned and approached them.
Rebecca donned her best intimidating look.

"Hey, Isabelle!" he said as he wrapped her in a hug. She could barely reach his chin, and Isabelle was tall for her age.

Rebecca wondered if Ryan was even the same age. She cleared her throat to ensure her presence was known.

Isabelle let go and looked at her. "Becky, this is Ryan. Remember I told you about him?"

Ryan extended his hand. "It's a pleasure to meet you. Isabelle has said so much about you."

"That's because I'm her sister, and we have a strong bond." She didn't shake his hand.

"Sorry if I came on too strong." Ryan let his hand drop. "Well, you have an amazing sister. She puts a smile on my face. She lights up any room."

"I don't need someone else to tell me she's amazing. I already know that. I also know she's really nice and can sometimes overlook the bad in people."

Ryan shifted his weight and jammed his hands into his pockets. He didn't seem to be enjoying the conversation at all, which was what Rebecca had hoped for. She didn't like anyone getting too comfortable with Isabelle. The boys back home were disgusting at times, and Rebecca didn't think Ryan would prove any different.

"Becky, are you okay?" Isabelle asked. She seemed confused by the situation.

"I'm fine. Just have fun, okay? I'm gonna go. I'll see you after class." She left the room, but, when the door closed, she turned to spy through the window. Ryan was talking to Isabelle. She didn't seem to like what he said as he pointed at the door. Rebecca assumed he was talking about her. The teacher called them to the dance floor, and they walked out of view. Rebecca felt that as long as Isabelle was inside the classroom, she was safe, so she left.

*****

The rest of November went by without any attacks again. It was as though the attacker might have thought Rebecca was too much to handle with her friends. Perhaps she had given up on it or was concocting another plan. Still, Rebecca didn't change her routine despite her grades falling. She and Morgan were both in the same boat, but Morgan didn't have an attacker stressing her out to the point she couldn't study.

In magiology, Rebecca was failing on nearly all her exams despite getting a good grasp on the idea of magic. It felt like Miss Stetson was purposely causing Rebecca to fail. She wanted to oust her for it, but she felt no one at Capitol Street would help her. Rebecca figured that Stetson and the school was afraid of Rebecca learning magic and then using it on others, yet Vanessa abused her own powers.

While Rebecca was giving an oral presentation on an English paper, she had felt her shoes untie themselves, and her tie had vividly loosened. Even though Mr. Wallace watched it all happen, he still deducted participation points for "dressing inappropriately." Vanessa smirked for the rest of the class period.

Something else on Rebecca's mind apart from the attacker was her looming seventeenth birthday. As the cold snow swept through Washington DC, things felt much better for her. She preferred the cold, and she enjoyed the sight of snow, but she had never seen so much dumped on one place.

December was also the month of Peacetime. Dr. Robertson had a history lecture about how it came to be. "As you all know, Peacetime is the celebration of kindness, compassion, family, and all of the good stuff. But does anyone know why it is celebrated in December?"

Andrew raised his hand, a common sight when a teacher had a question. "It's because when they signed the peace treaty, not everyone could just stop fighting. Battles took place so far away, it would have taken weeks to send the message that it was all over, thus more people would have died. So, the Peace Queen made it snow for thirty days straight, forcing the soldiers to bunker down and spend time with their comrades. It stopped all the fighting in the world almost immediately."

"Exactly," Dr. Robertson said. "And, as it snows now, it should be a reminder to us that whatever beef you may have with others, you could be putting your energy into other things. Cherish the moments with those you love and not brood on those you hate."

The bell rang, and Dr. Robertson dismissed the class. Rebecca met up with Morgan and Andrew outside the classroom. Morgan was carrying her plant, claiming it would be too cold to stay away from body heat. It had wrapped its vines around her.

"Only a few weeks before winter break!" Morgan chimed as she petted the plant's leaves. "Any plans?"

"Probably nothing of interest back home," Andrew said. "If I could, I would just stay here during the break."

"I guess Kate will have something planned for me and Issy," Rebecca said.

"My parents are hosting a big family dinner. So many cousins. I really don't think I can handle it," Morgan said.

Rebecca was slightly annoyed her friends didn't want to go home, yet she would give anything to return to her own in England. She even missed her childish brother Ray and his antics.

"So, Rebecca," Morgan continued, "I saw a circle on your calendar for the twelfth. What's that for?"

"Oh, Issy circled that for my birthday." She wished she had said it was for homework or something, because Morgan's eyes lit up.

"You mean your birthday is in four days, and you didn't bother to tell your best friends?"

Rebecca rolled her eyes. "It's not that big of a deal."

"If I'm not mistaken, seventeen is the adult age in Europe?" Andrew asked.

"Not here, which is why I'm not worried about it."

"Becca, we are so throwing you a party," Morgan said. "A small one, but you need a cake, some friends—and not just me and Andrew—maybe a movie to watch. We can do it in the commons on the first floor."

"Okay, a chocolate cake does sound delicious, but what other friends do I have besides you two and Isabelle?"

"I think Regan would come, and perhaps Isabelle can bring Faith," Andrew suggested.

"And, of course, Alvin will come," Morgan teased.

"Doubt it. He's still probably too interested in Vanessa to worry about me."

Rebecca had not been on speaking terms with Alvin since the Halloween party. Anytime Alvin tried to chat with her, Rebecca only made small talk. She wanted to sound as uninteresting as possible. She even kept Alexis Black as her culinary arts partner.

"I know you still like him," Morgan said, "so ask him to the party or you get no cake."

"Now that's cruel."

Morgan grinned.

"I think you should also invite Alexis," Andrew said. "I know she's not the type to hang out with people, but she might appreciate that someone wants to be her friend."

"I agree," Morgan said. "She's got it in pretty bad with Vanessa's gang ever since we all started at Capitol Street, but I'm not sure why."

Rebecca, Morgan, and Andrew finalized their list of people to invite. Rebecca asked Isabelle and Faith during their walk from class, and they were both on board; however, Isabelle had a special request. "Is it okay if Ryan comes along?"

"Er" was all that came from Rebecca's mouth.

"I know you don't know him as well as I do, but I think you'll like him once you do."

"He's not as bad as you think," Faith added.

"Alright then," Rebecca said. She still didn't like it, but if Faith approved, then perhaps Ryan was okay. But Rebecca noted the choice of words Faith had used—Not as bad as you think. That told Rebecca there was still bad in him.

Later on, outside of English class, Rebecca and Morgan approached Regan about the birthday party.

"Will there be plenty of hot chocolate?" Regan asked.

"There might be," Morgan said. "I think the commons keeps that stocked pretty good this time of the year."

"Perhaps we should hide it to keep anyone else from using it," Regan suggested.

Rebecca was a little surprised at Regan for suggesting to sneak something around, but perhaps she considered hiding hot chocolate a misdemeanor.

During culinary arts, Rebecca sat with Alexis, who wasn't in a talkative mood as usual. It was almost like Rebecca didn't have a partner and that they did their own work instead of working together.

"Hey, Alexis. I've got something to ask you."

"What is it?" Alexis asked, not sounding in the slightest bit interested.

"I'm having a birthday party, and I was hoping you'd like to come." Rebecca watched Alexis, who didn't say anything initially as she worked on her recipe.

"Why do you want me to come?" she finally asked when Rebecca didn't expect an answer.

"Well, you and I have been partners in this class for a while now, and, after getting to know you, I thought you'd be a cool person to hang out with."

"Cool? I'm far from that, and we hardly speak, so how have you gotten to know me? No, you shouldn't want to hang out with me."

"Why not?"

"Because … you're better off without me going."

Rebecca bit her lip. She didn't understand why Alexis was being so vague, but Rebecca had tried, and she said no. She wasn't about to press the issue.

After class, it was time to ask Alvin to the party. She felt more nervous than ever about talking to him. Would he be mad at her for ignoring him for so long? She had a feeling he would say no.

Before she got up from her seat, however, Alexis took Rebecca's hand and put something inside it. Rebecca did not raise her hand to look. Whatever it was, Alexis was trying to be discreet about it.

Rebecca returned her attention to Alvin. She had to catch up to him, even running down the hallway.

"Alvin!"

People stared as Alvin stopped. Rebecca didn't want the attention around them, and thankfully, it looked as though everyone carried on.

"Oh, hey, Rebecca."

"Hey, I, er. I have, um, a question for you."

Alvin raised an eyebrow.

"Would you like to come to my birthday party this Saturday?"

Alvin seemed surprised and deep in thought, like he was debating whether he wanted to go. "Um, I'm not sure. I just, well, you seem to have been upset with me lately, and so, it's kind of got me upset with you."

"What? No, I haven't been."

"You haven't spoken no more than two words to me since the Halloween party, and I'm not even sure why."

Rebecca's heart rate increased. She felt jumpy and shaky. "Well … you did leave with Vanessa while we were dancing."

"Vanessa? She had to talk to me about student government. She's the vice—"

"I don't care what she is, but I thought we had a thing going, and you completely ruined it when you abandoned me."

"I ruined it? I did a lot of things for you that night to make you comfortable. Did you forget that?"

Rebecca didn't want to talk to Alvin anymore. She had nothing else to say. She turned her back on him and walked in the opposite direction, trying to hold back tears. A hand rested on her shoulder, and she tried to jerk it away.

"Leave me alone!" she shouted, turning around thinking it was Alvin. "Oh, I'm so sorry."

"It's fine," Morgan said. "I saw what happened. Don't blame yourself."

"I'm not. He was the one being completely stupid."

"Well, I guess now we know he's not coming, but what about Alexis?"

Rebecca remembered the piece of paper and unfolded it from her hand. "She said she'll come. Why didn't she just say this in class? She told me she couldn't come."

"I told you something is odd about her."

*****

Rebecca now knew who was coming, but despite having all her friends at the party, she was still upset about Alvin not attending. She couldn't understand how it was in any way her fault.

Morgan had to remind her not to beat herself up over it before the party started. When Andrew found out, he suggested to not worry about relationships, because they just impeded one's goals. Morgan seemed upset by his advice but didn't say anything. Instead, she had her plant expand its vines to create a cool party-decoration pattern along the space between the commons' walls and ceiling.

The party had begun, and everyone arrived, as they had promised. Even Alexis attended, but she looked out of place. She made it seem like she had accidentally stumbled into the commons, and she kept her distance from the crowd.

Rebecca sat beside Alexis while Morgan and Regan were occupied discussing gladius dueling. "What made you decide to come?"

"I wanted to, but I couldn't say it in front of Cassandra and Sheila. It's a long story, but I used to be their friends before we got to Capitol Street."

"What makes you worried about them finding out you went to the party?"

Alexis did not divulge any further, and Rebecca didn't press it anymore, but she still insisted that Alexis come join the party instead of sitting alone. Alexis hesitated, but she relinquished when Rebecca offered a hot cup of cocoa.

Ryan arrived and Isabelle ran to hug him. It pained Rebecca to see it, but she didn't want to ruin anything for her sister. She would keep an eye on him the whole night, however.

Everything seemed to be going well. Everyone was laughing and sipping hot chocolate. Morgan and Regan brought out the chocolate cake with turquoise-blue frosting, which they had made together in culinary arts.

"To match your hair," Morgan noted.

For the first time, Rebecca felt like she had a proper birthday party. Never had there been more than her sisters and brothers around. Of course, Lucy had always attended them ever since they had been friends, and Rebecca's mother would make a cake for her too. And while she missed her family tonight, it felt like she was closer to home than she had ever been since being in America. Everyone here attended because they had a choice and they chose too. It was even her new friends' idea to throw the party.

Rebecca had to sit through an embarrassing "Happy Birthday" song before she could blow out any candles. Once they finished, she bent her head to make a wish, but, before she could finish, the doors to the commons burst open. Rebecca turned to see Vanessa and Cassandra wielding a sword while Sheila had a bow and a quiver of arrows.

Vanessa surveyed the party, then her gaze fell onto Rebecca.

"I hope you wished for a quick execution when my father finally sends you back home."

"What do you want, Vanessa?" Rebecca asked.

"Besides wanting you out of my school, Morgan to lose weight, Andrew to flunk out, and to get my friend back"—Vanessa glanced at Alexis—"I want this party to end right now."

"I'm glad you care so much about my health," Morgan said, "but you can't stop this party."

"Where did you get those swords?" Regan asked.

"Found them in one of the old basements. Did you know this school was built on top of an underground prison from the colonial days? It's pretty cool."

"Some old skeletons are down there too," Sheila said. "Maybe you'll find a long lost relative, Andrew."

"And you couldn't find some of your own?"

"The Waldgraves have never been trash. We are descendants of old African royalty," Sheila said proudly.

Vanessa stepped forward and raised her sword to a table nearby. She slid it across, knocking off cups of hot chocolate. "Tut-tut. Your party has led to spilled drinks. With all this mess, you should lose your commons privileges."

"Vanessa," Regan said, "If you don't put those swords back where you got them, I will suspend all three of you from dueling club."

"Shut your mouth!" Vanessa removed a roll of duct tape and threw it at Regan. With a wave of her hand, the tape unraveled and wrapped Regan multiple times across her mouth, eyes, arms, and legs She toppled, and Isabelle and Faith tried to help remove it.

Ryan charged at Vanessa, but she took the remaining duct tape, tripped him and kept him stuck to the floor.

"That's enough!" Rebecca said as she stepped forward. She didn't believe Vanessa would do anything with her sword, but she raised it to Rebecca as she approached. The tip rested an inch from her nose. Sheila had raised her bow on Andrew, and Cassandra kept Morgan at bay.

"This party is over and so is your terror," Vanessa said. "You will not keep being a threat to me and my school."

"You're out of your mind, Ness," Alexis said from afar.

"Says the one who's crazy enough to stop being friends with me and join with the enemy. I told Daddy we should have kept a closer eye on you and your—" Vanessa screamed as she dropped the sword and reached for her shoulder. A star blade was sticking in her.

Nobody knew where it had come from, but it started an outbreak in the commons. Cassandra changed her focus to Rebecca and swung her sword. Rebecca ducked and scooped Vanessa's blade, and the girls clashed.

Isabelle screamed, and Faith came forward to get her out of harm's way. Meanwhile, Sheila was firing her arrows at Andrew, who was trying to throw mugs and whatever else he could find. An arrow nearly got him, when he used an encyclopedia to stop it in its tracks.

"Leave him alone, you slut!" Morgan shouted as a vine crawled up Sheila's leg and tripped her to fall face first. Morgan ran over and kicked the bow out of her hands. Rebecca swore she'd heard the crunch of a finger being stepped on.

Rebecca forced Cassandra to the ground, but since this was no sanctioned gladius duel, Cassandra saw no reason to stop. This was her mistake, as Rebecca planted her foot on her face before she could grab her sword.

Vanessa, Cassandra, and Sheila all tucked tail and sprinted from the commons. Rebecca, standing tall over the mess, dared them to return before turning to check on Isabelle. She was in Faith's arms, but she broke from her grasp to hold onto Rebecca.

Faith joined Andrew to help get Regan and Ryan out of the tape, which seemed to be coming off a lot easier. Morgan believed Vanessa had kept her magic concentrated on them, which was why she didn't use hers on Rebecca.

The commons door opened again. Rebecca drew Vanessa's sword in its direction, but it wasn't Vanessa or her friends. It was Alvin.

Everyone returned to the party by either cleaning the mess or socializing. Rebecca stood still with Isabelle at her side as Alvin approached them.

"Hey," he said then pointed at the sword. "That's a cool birthday gift."

"Yeah, Vanessa gave it to me."

Alvin looked confused, but he shook his head. "I'm sorry about Halloween. I really did want to come back to you, and I tried, but you were gone, and I felt terrible. I thought you were done with me, and I was mad about it. I wasn't mad with you though. I was mad with myself. So, I'm very sorry about earlier this week as well."

Rebecca looked at Isabelle, who smiled at her and Alvin. Rebecca faced the boy. "Apology accepted, but I'm still mad at you for this week."

"If it takes time, I'm okay with that."

"And I'm also sorry for not talking to you for the past month," Rebecca added.

"I wouldn't have wanted to talk to me either, so no worries." Alvin laughed.

Normalcy returned to the party, and Rebecca finally could properly blow out her birthday cake candles. Who said you can't have your cake and eat it too? Rebecca was able to get rid of Vanessa and win Alvin back. It was now a perfect birthday party.

Traditional Physical Symbol

Chapter 9

N o one knew who had thrown the star blade at Vanessa, but word of it had spread around the school, and she dared anyone to come near her shoulder to look at it. She seemed to be walking awkwardly too. Perhaps she was in pain but hadn't told anyone what or how it had happened.

Unfortunately, it was a short-lived celebration, because classes had ended for Peacetime. Students had no interest in what was happening at Capitol Street Academy, as they all focused on their plans for when they arrived home.

The buses lined up at the front gates as students clambered on with their luggage. Rebecca said goodbye to Morgan and Andrew, who were all boarding different buses going in their own direction.

Rebecca planned to sit with her sister, but, as they stepped onto their bus, Isabelle found Faith. The seats were made for just two people, and, as much as Rebecca would like to tell them to make room for her, she didn't want to be awkward, so she searched for an open seat. The only one left was beside someone she wasn't expecting.

Lucy stared out the window, not noticing who was gazing at her. Rebecca thought she looked like she was thinking deeply, something she had never seen Lucy do. She had always been more about action than thinking. It was actually kind of cute the way she was gazing at the school, her copper brown eyes piercing the campus.

Rebecca sat without saying a word. Instead, she stared at her thumbs and twiddled them together.

Lucy turned to see who had sat down, stared for a moment then returned to looking out the window.

Rebecca wished she could have seen her facial expression, but Rebecca didn't dare look back.

They sat in silence for a long time. Everyone else laughed and teased and discussed their drama. At the first bus stop just outside Baltimore, Rebecca contemplated moving to a different seat now that a few were unoccupied, but she didn't move.

"I guess you did want to sit with me?" Lucy said.

Surprised, Rebecca faced Lucy. "Actually, no I didn't."

"But you're still here. Why don't you take another seat?"

"Because ..." Rebecca harrumphed.

Lucy returned to looking out the window, and Rebecca spied an empty seat just down the aisle.

"How was your birthday party after Vanessa left?" Lucy asked.

"What do you mean?"

"Well, after I threw that ninja star at her, I was hoping you would have fun after her crash."

Rebecca faced Lucy again. "You did what?"

Lucy hesitated. "I was coming to see you for your birthday. You know I've never missed one since we've known each other. It just didn't feel right to not see you on your birthday."

"That still doesn't explain why you attacked Vanessa."

"Well, I was outside the room when she walked in, and I saw what she was doing. She pissed me off, so I snuck in and chucked it at her. I was actually going to give that star to you for your birthday."

Rebecca couldn't believe it, but, at the same time, she knew the only person it would make sense to do such a thing was Lucy. Their friendship had formed because Lucy had stood up to one of Rebecca's bullies back home.

"So why didn't you come in after Vanessa left?"

"I figured once you saw Vanessa, I would have ruined your whole party."

The bus crossed from Maryland into Pennsylvania. Their next stop was Philadelphia. Rebecca grew tired of seeing the cityscapes. One of the benefits to living back home was that the Warren Estate sat in the middle of nowhere, and, at night, the stars would beautifully radiate.

"You know, if you still wanted to be friends, you could have asked."

"Ask?" Lucy faked a laugh. "You were the one who had ended it." Lucy stood and sat a few rows ahead of Rebecca.

Rebecca watched from behind as Lucy lowered her head. Rebecca wanted to talk to her, but she felt stuck to her seat. She wasn't sure what she would say.

Instead, Rebecca laid down and drifted off to sleep.

*****

"Becky! Get up! You gotta get up!"

Rebecca's eyes opened to darkness. Hours must have passed. Isabelle stood over her from the seat in front. It was difficult to see her expression, but her voice sounded excited.

Rebecca sat up and looked around. They were stopped at a bustling street with lights on every lamp, car, and window. Rebecca had just seen Lucy exit the bus, her short brown hair bouncing as she descended the steps. That was the only activity Rebecca could see inside the bus though.

"What is it?" she asked Isabelle.

"Come on! This is our stop. And look who's with Kate!"

Rebecca peered out the window at the sidewalk. First, her eyes had to focus after the long nap. She found her tall, light-brown haired cousin standing beside a man with curly blond hair sticking out of the sides of a toboggan.

Rebecca backed from the window and sprinted off the bus. She studied the two adults and froze, thinking she was seeing things. "Blake?"

The young man grinned, and Rebecca darted right to him. Her arms clenched around him into a hug. Suddenly, she felt all her troubles vanish. Blake had also gripped Rebecca tightly, and it made her feel like she was still loved and missed. They didn't break apart for a good minute. Isabelle had also joined them, and they stayed huddled together while Kate collected the girls' luggage.

Finally, Blake broke them apart to look at them. Rebecca had a clearer look at him too. Her godbrother never had facial hair before, and now it was growing wildly. For being just in his mid-twenties, his face looked rugged, and his eyes appeared as tired as an old man.

"It's been too long," he finally said with a smile, which Rebecca believed he hadn't done for quite some time. It seemed to make him look full of life.

"I've missed you," Rebecca said.

"We have so much to tell you," Isabelle spouted.

"I'm sure you do, and I can't wait to hear it all. And yes, I can't express how much I've missed you both as well."

They all finally got into Kate's car and drove for about an hour. Isabelle talked most of the way and told Blake how Capitol Street had been for them. Rebecca was fine with Isabelle doing all the talking. She and Blake understood their conversations would be different from the ones that involved their sister.

At dinner in Kate's kitchen, Isabelle asked the first question Rebecca already had lined up for him. "What's happening back home?"

"Well, things are going … They're okay. We're winning the fight."

"What about Mum and Dad? And Ray and Bianca and Aunt Aimee?"

"They're all okay." Blake scratched his beard, which prompted Rebecca with a question of her own.

"Why are you growing that thing? It looks terrible."

Blake laughed. "It's keeping my identity secret. Everyone who is looking for me still thinks I look like a kid."

"So, you're kind of like a superhero?" Isabelle asked.

"Exactly. So, don't tell everyone I'm here. I'm not supposed to be, but it's Peacetime. I couldn't imagine you two being alone this time of year. No offense, Kate."

"None taken," she said as she raised a wine glass to sip.

To Kate's surprise, no one hesitated to go to bed by the end of the night. Blake had decided to sleep on the couch, while the girls bunked in their bedroom and Kate in hers. When everything sounded as though no one would wake up, Rebecca quietly slipped from her bed and tiptoed from her bedroom to find Blake, who was sitting up.

"I thought you went to sleep," he whispered.

Rebecca rolled her eyes with a grin.

Blake stood and beckoned Rebecca to follow him. They stepped into the brightly lit apartment complex hallway and walked.

"So, how are things really going back home?" Rebecca asked.

"You must have been dying to ask that question ever since Issy asked. But not here. Let's get somewhere where we won't be overheard. I really am growing this beard for the reasons I mentioned earlier."

Blake led Rebecca into the stairwell, and they climbed to the top floor, where a ladder stood with a lock keeping it unreachable for anyone to climb. It didn't stop Blake though, as he extended his hand at it and twisted it. There was a struggle, by the look on his face, but the lock soon snapped, and the ladder was free. Rebecca gaped at him.

"I learned a trick or two since the unrest started." He smirked. "From my understanding, they're teaching you magic too?" He gestured for Rebecca to climb the ladder first.

"Yeah, but I'm nowhere near what you just did," Rebecca said as she started up.

"What can you do?"

"Nothing. I'm terrible at it."

Rebecca opened the hatch above her, and a field of twinkling stars greeted her. She paused to gaze at them. Washington D.C. never had a view like this.

The two found a spot to lay down to survey the night sky. Rebecca had forgotten why they were even up here, but Blake sighed loudly. "Things are not going well back home. Mathias is trying everything he can to get an army into France to find your parents. Thankfully, our mums have enough money to keep them from going that way, but the civil unrest has completely destroyed England."

"What does Mathias want from us? There must be more to it than just because we have money and fame."

"If there is, he hasn't made it clear, but he is still trying everything he can to get you and Isabelle arrested too. I actually think he wants you two more than the rest of us."

Rebecca sat up to think. She wasn't sure if she wanted to tell Blake about the incidents on campus. She didn't think he could do anything at this point, given that it always happened at school, and she was afraid they would catch him if he stayed in America trying to help her.

"Why don't you let me come back with you? I want to fight," she said. "If they're trying to turn on us here, then Issy and I won't have any protection."

"You do have protection. Didn't you say earlier that Lucy was here? And what about Morgan and Andrew?"

"Lucy and I aren't friends anymore. I … screwed that up. And I doubt Morgan and Andrew will stick out their necks to protect me."

"With the way you talked about them, they seem like they care, and you should fix that about Luce. You two have always been great for each other."

"But she used me."

"Well, you used me to get away with sneaking out of the house with her."

"Yeah, but that's different."

"Is it?"

Rebecca couldn't think of a reply.

"Look, whatever problems you have with your friends, it's nothing in the long run. If they're not hurting you, it's things you can work out. Right now, you need your best friend more than ever, because this world is changing—and not for the better. It's good to have someone loyal in your corner."

Rebecca nodded.

"Promise me you'll fix things with Lucy."

"I promise."

Clouds rolled between them and the stars. Slowly, the sky darkened.

Blake sat up and sighed. "There's one more thing. Your mum's disease has worsened."

"Oh …" Rebecca trembled. "How bad is it?"

"She can't walk on her own power. There's been a big fight about it recently. What happens if Mathias finds us? Do we leave her behind, or do we stay and fight?"

"Stay and fight, of course!"

"Your dad and her both say differently. They say to leave her behind so the rest of us have a chance."

"They, or just dad?"

"It was actually your mum who said it first. I don't think it'll come to that though. We recently moved to the old Bedel Estate ruins in Paris. There's a second basement only a Bedel would know about."

"Good thing both our fathers fancied the ladies of that family," Rebecca joked.

A piercing scream came from below. Rebecca and Blake looked at each other, and they knew who it was. They shot up and ran for the hatch. Down the ladder. Down the stairs. Through the hallway. Into the apartment. The girls' bedroom light was on.

Rebecca and Blake blasted into it to find Kate cradling Isabelle.

Capitol Street Academy

Traditional Natural Symbol

Chapter 10

Rebecca rushed to the bed, and Isabelle reached out for her. The girls clung together for a moment, and everything seemed to be fine.

"I had a bad dream," Isabelle muttered. "And then you weren't there, and I got scared she took you and Blake away."

"We're right here," Rebecca said. "Who did you think tried to take us?"

"That person who attacked us with the arrow."

"You mean Annabelle Alexandria?" Blake asked as he joined the girls on the bed.

Rebecca lifted her head from Isabelle's shoulder to look at Blake.

"I heard about the attack. Mathias has been trying to get America's president to hand you over, but I believe he's sent someone here in secret to kidnap you two. Alexandria makes the most sense to do it."

"Who is she?" Rebecca asked.

"She got locked up last year trying to kill one of our family's friends, the Perrys. I don't know the full story, but I think they screwed her out of a job. When Mathias took the throne, he claimed there was an error in the investigation, and she was freed. Now she works for him as one of the castle's highest security guards. She's a top-notch archer."

"And nobody thought that was suspicious?" Kate asked.

"The civil unrest was already on. Nobody cared about it. I only know of it because the Perrys were hiding with us, and they told us when they found it in a newspaper."

"So Andrew was right," Rebecca said. "Someone is trying to kidnap us." She stood and started packing her and Isabelle's things.

"What are you doing?" Kate asked.

"We aren't safe here. Not in America. We need to go back home or at least to where Mum is. Kate, you should come too. That woman probably knows who you are by now."

Blake grabbed Rebecca's arm to keep her from zipping up her luggage. She looked into his eyes, which stared back with assurance.

"Becca, you are much safer here. It's like I told you. You have people here to protect you."

"If I do, then why haven't they told me? Where were they when that arrow hit Alvin? One that was supposed to hit me. Where were they when Annabelle attacked me and Morgan?"

Blake seemed frustrated. He opened his mouth, closed it, then said, "Look, I'm not supposed to say if you don't know, but … trust me. Someone is there protecting you."

Rebecca didn't know what to say or do. She did trust him that someone was supposed to be there to protect her and Isabelle, but she didn't trust the person. Ever since she got to Capitol Street, nobody had stepped forward and tried to tell her that they were there to safeguard them. It certainly wasn't Morgan or Andrew. They were just kids like her and Isabelle. Lucy may have protected Rebecca from bullies back at their old school, but she doubted her former best friend was skilled enough to stop a criminal who had intentions to kill.

The Bancrofts, who were just as rich as the Warrens, hated Rebecca's guts for being at their school. The only other person she could think of was a teacher, but none of them had stood up to help her either. Whoever it was, they were no longer interested in being a bodyguard for the Warrens.

Nevertheless, Rebecca couldn't argue against Blake's wishes. She trusted him to make the right decisions for her, even if it was the same plans her father had arranged. Rebecca felt that Blake didn't like the girls being by themselves, but perhaps he didn't feel it was his place to contradict his godfather.

But Blake had been more like a parent to Rebecca than her father ever had. It was Blake who took Rebecca on camping and city trips to see the world. It was he who showed Rebecca how to find herself and taught her things a dad should. He helped her with homework and demonstrated how to be a good person. When she needed time to spend with someone, he was there.

Rebecca released the luggage and dropped her hands to her side. Blake smiled then scooped her up and placed her on the bed beside Isabelle. "I'll tell you what. When this is all over, we'll open a bakery together right in the heart of Paris. The three of us."

"A bakery?" Isabelle repeated. "But you don't know how to bake."

"Oh. Well, I can run all of the management stuff and be the official taste tester."

"We'll never make a profit with you in that position," Rebecca said. Everyone laughed before they returned to bed.

*****

Throughout Peacetime, the Warrens spent the season together, having laughs and telling stories. Rebecca convinced Blake to trim his beard. He now no longer looked homeless. His eyes seemed to be less war weary as the days passed too. Kate arranged for them to all go out to dinner at a nice restaurant on the night before they had to return to Capitol Street.

Blake, however, was not staying forever, and Rebecca dreaded the day of returning to Capitol Street. Her godbrother had arranged to board a France-bound plane that same morning. Kate drove them all to the airport. Blake didn't want them all to come, because it might draw attention, but Rebecca and Isabelle insisted. Not only that, but Kate planned to go to their bus station after dropping off Blake, so it only made sense they came along anyway.

They arrived at the Albany International Airport, which was not the same one Rebecca and Isabelle had landed at when they had arrived in the state of New York. This was good, because Albany, despite being the state's capital, was a bit smaller than the other, which meant fewer people would be looking for him.

As a precaution, Blake gave Rebecca a grey snapback hat to help hide her blue hair, and Isabelle wore the toboggan he had worn the day they reunited. Having them inside and out in the open would have revealed his identity.

It never occurred to Rebecca until they walked inside how Blake had snuck into America, but Blake showed an airport attendant a ticket to Paris along with a visa for the name Melvin C. Selrah. Blake spouted his best French accent too, which was stellar—as it should be since his mother, as well as Rebecca's and Isabelle's, were both pureblood French. Rebecca even decided to speak in French as well to play it off even more.

"Your. Gate. Is. That. Way," the attendant said very loudly and making hand gestures as though Blake had no idea how to speak English. When they got out of earshot, Rebecca and Blake both laughed.

"She really fell for that one, didn't she, Issy?" Rebecca asked. Isabelle didn't respond though. Rebecca turned to look at her sister. Her smile disappeared; Isabelle was not there. Rebecca halted to look around.

Blonde and pink hair whipped around the corner of a hallway, the toboggan falling off.

"Issy!" Rebecca shouted and ran in her sister's direction. She reached the hallway and looked down it.

A woman was dragging Isabelle.

Rebecca rushed for them. As she got closer, she noticed a strip of tape was gagging Isabelle. Rebecca's footsteps hammered on the floor and echoed off the walls. They were the only three in the hallway, as far as she could tell.

The woman looked back and quickened her pace. She was now carrying the kicking Isabelle and hurried on.

Rebecca was closing in on them though.

The woman and Isabelle went through a door, and Rebecca made it just before it closed completely.

"Stop right there!" Rebecca yelled.

"Of course," the woman said. She lazily halted and dropped Isabelle onto the floor. The woman put her foot on top of Isabelle's back to keep her in place.

Tears streaked Isabelle's cheeks with fear.

"Now let her go," Rebecca demanded.

"Sorry, kid. That's where I draw the line. How about instead you join your sister, and I'll take you home? Surely you want to go back, right?"

"You're Annabelle, aren't you? You've been attacking us all school year."

"You got me," Annabelle said with a laugh, "but now I got you." Annabelle removed a switchblade knife from her belt. Her other hand retrieved a pair of handcuffs. She reached down and placed one end on Isabelle's wrist, pulled her up and secured her to a rail. "I'll make this real simple for you. Turn yourself in to King Mathias and you won't have to worry about dying tonight."

"You won't kill me. Mathias needs me and my sister for leverage."

"Actually, the only one he wants is your sister. I've only been trying to capture you to make sweet little Issy come to me. But now I don't need you. You're just in the way, and I'll make quick work of you."

Annabelle approached Rebecca, who backed all the way to the wall beside the door. Annabelle came closer, manhandling the knife. Rebecca didn't know what to do. Bullies were one thing, someone trying to kill her was another.

Rebecca had no ideas, and she panicked. She put her hand on the wall and closed her eyes, thinking this was it for her. She heard Isabelle squeal, and Rebecca felt some kind of handle and pulled it out of desperation.

A fire siren blared. Rebecca opened her eyes to see the water sprinklers were spitting right at Annabelle. This was the chance to run. The only escape route Rebecca saw was over numerous stacked crates. One hop after another, all she had to do was keep Annabelle busy long enough for the authorities to arrive, but Annabelle was quick to follow behind her. Rebecca jumped from crate to crate. She pushed on one to knock it over to keep Annabelle out of reach.

She fell to the ground with a clatter of wood and metal. Rebecca maneuvered toward Isabelle and tried her best to free her. The cuffs were too tight, so Rebecca tried to calm her down. "Issy. Look at me. I'll get you out of this. I swear."

Isabelle was still frightened, even more so than before Rebecca spoke to her.

"I swear it. You'll be—"

Rebecca was nearly hit with something metal, and it crashed along the bar that held Isabelle. Rebecca ducked as Annabelle now wielded a sword. Rebecca didn't know what to do now. The blade was inches from her throat.

Someone latched onto Annabelle's neck and tried to bring her to her knees. It was Blake. "Get Isabelle out of here! Find something to break her free!"

Rebecca watched for a moment as Blake struggled to drag Annabelle to the floor. She scanned the mess made from the toppled crates and spotted a pile of swords. Rebecca rushed to them, grabbed one and hurried back to see Annabelle free herself from Blake's grasp.

Rebecca charged. Annabelle rolled out of the way, and their swords clashed. Annabelle was well trained, and Rebecca could hold her own, but she knew she couldn't maintain it; Annabelle was stronger.

"You're good," Annabelle said, "but you're not good enough."

She kicked Rebecca onto the floor, with her blade falling from her hand. Annabelle stood over her.

Rebecca closed her eyes. It was over.

Annabelle grunted, and Rebecca looked. Blake had tackled her again, hugging her so she couldn't extend her sword and do damage. She released it and pounded on Blake's back. "Enough of this nonsense!"

Blake bellowed as he released Annabelle. He rolled off her while holding his side where Annabelle had stuck her switchblade.

Rebecca cried out, but her wails felt empty.

The blade embedded farther into his side as Annabelle rolled Blake to his back, and she struck his chest.

Doors all around them banged open as police crashed in. Annabelle stood and ran for it.

They fired arrows at her, but none seemed to hit their target.

Rebecca hurried to Blake, who was breathing heavily. She looked down at him and he up at her.

"I-I-I can pull it out," Rebecca stammered. "Will that help?"

"You ... can't ... help ... me."

"No. I need you!" Rebecca squeezed his hand tight as her godbrother's own became heavier to hold. "Please don't ..."

"Listen ..." Blake heaved. "Talk ... to ... Stetson."

"Blake, please ..."

"I'll ... miss you."

Blake's chest didn't move any longer. No life remained in his blue eyes, and his hand collapsed to the floor.

Rebecca fell onto his body and tears fell onto him. She didn't want to move from this place. She wanted to stay and be with Blake.

A set of hands grabbed Rebecca, and she jerked them away, but they kept coming.

"No! Leave me alone! Get away from me!"

Hands pinned her wrists to her lower back, and she felt something grip them—handcuffs. They dragged her away from Blake.

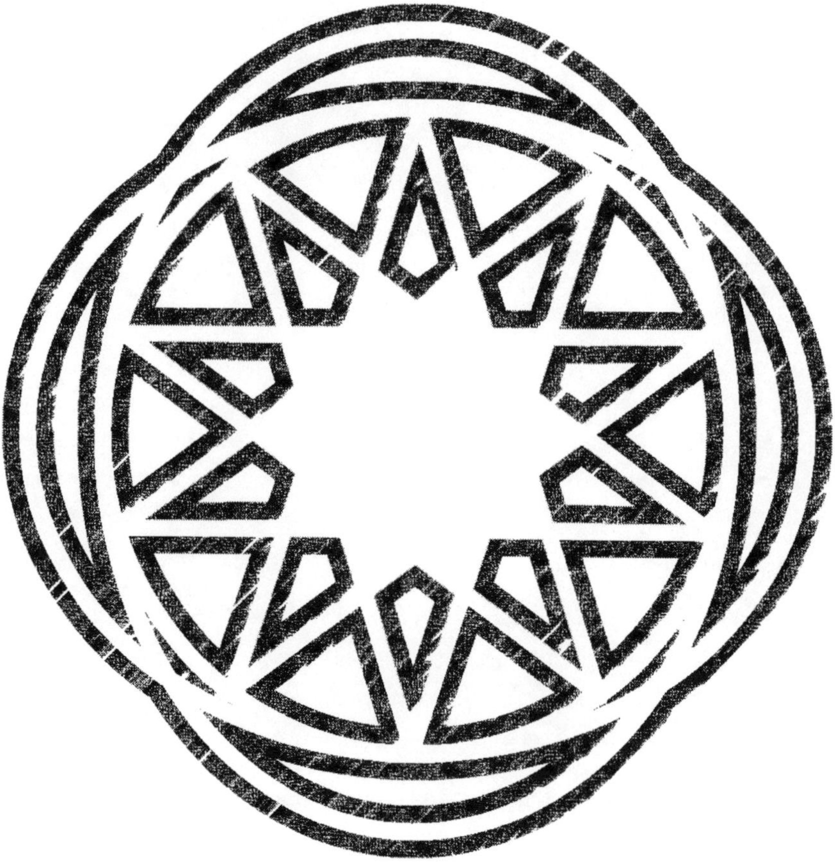

Traditional Spiritual Symbol

Chapter 11

A low buzz filled the dead air of a squared room. A single light was on inside, and there were no windows except for a glass that acted as a mirror. It was likely people could see into the room from the other side.

Rebecca watched herself closely. She looked deranged and broken. Her cuffed hands were speckled with dried blood as they sat on top of a desk. Her hair was more disheveled than ever before. The strip of blue was accompanied by red. She stared hard into her own reflection. It was the only person she had in the room with her, and it was the only one she wanted to strangle.

She didn't move though—not because her ankles and wrists were chained to the desk and chair, but because she didn't know what she would do to herself. She kept replaying the image of her godbrother dying right in front of her. She had already cried for him, but now she wanted to avenge him.

The door opened, and several people entered. Rebecca was met with two guards and a man. Rebecca didn't recognize him, but she didn't care to learn who he was. The only thing on her mind was finding Annabelle Alexandria and kill her.

"Rebecca Warren," he said provocatively. "What a shame your last name has become to the world."

Rebecca said nothing.

The man placed his hands onto the desk and leaned in front of her. "You're covered in your own godbrother's blood—your godbrother who wasn't supposed to be in America, your brother who the King of England desperately wanted to locate. It doesn't look good for you to be found with him, given the trust this nation has given you."

Rebecca remained silent. She hoped they would send her back to England. It might improve her chances of finding Annabelle and killing her and King Mathias both.

"It also doesn't look good for your sister. Pity, because she probably really didn't have anything to do with it. But I could be surprised."

"Where's Isabelle?" Rebecca gritted. It clicked in her head—forget Annabelle; she had to find her sister.

She tried to stand. It was her first movement since being in the room, but she quickly remembered she wasn't going anywhere.

"There we go," the man said, as if this was the reaction he wanted out of her. "Don't worry. She's fine … for now. But that'll all depend on how you answer my next questions."

"I'm not talking to anyone until I see my sister!"

The door opened again, and this time, a woman and another man entered. Rebecca noticed a red, white, and blue flag with a white star in the middle pinned on the man's jacket collar.

"That's enough, Bancroft," the woman said. "You're no longer heading this investigation."

Rebecca now recognized the man in front of her. She had seen him on the news many times warning how much of a danger she and Isabelle were to America. It was Vanessa's father, Victor Bancroft.

"What the hell do you mean by that?" Mr. Bancroft asked.

"Calm down, Mr. Bancroft," the flag pin man said. He too looked familiar. "Miss Evans will be taking over. I must take you off of it, given the sensitive situation and your personal beliefs."

"But, as secretary of state, I oversee foreign affairs. An illegal man was in this country posing a threat to us, and she was aiding him."

"You have no proof of that," Miss Evans said. "Now get out of my interrogation room."

"Blake Taylor was undocumented and here illegally. That's more than proof."

"I meant by him posing a threat. Did he kill or attack anyone?"

"I'm sure he had plans. Even so, you can't deny he had no business here. Not even you can stand against that, Mr. President."

"I believe his business here was simply to see his family for Peacetime," the president said. "People will do anything to see their loved ones happy, as I'm sure you know better than anyone else."

Victor Bancroft didn't move. "Even if I'm not heading the investigation, I still have the choice to stay and ask questions."

"Very well then," Miss Evans said. She looked at the two guards. "You two can leave. I will not use intimidation tactics."

They both left the room in a hurry.

Miss Evans faced Rebecca. "We're sorry about that. I'm sure the last thing you want is someone accusing your brother, but one thing I will agree with Mr. Bancroft is that him being here is certainly alarming for the United States."

"Where is my sister?"

"A medical team is examining her. She's safe."

"And she'll stay that way, including you," the president said.

"I want to see her."

"You'll get to, but we need you to talk to us first," Miss Evans said. "Let's start with introductions. My name is Melanie Evans, and this is Gregory Oppenheimer, the United States President."

"I'm sorry about your loss," President Oppenheimer said. "I'm certain he came here with good intentions."

"He came to see me and Issy for Peacetime, as you said. That was it."

"Oh, come on," Mr. Bancroft retorted. "We all know you haven't had communication with anyone from the outside. Your brother told you things crucial to ending the civil unrest in your country, and you need to tell us."

"If he did tell me anything, I wouldn't tell you."

"Conspiracy against the country," Mr. Bancroft called out.

"Silence, you fool," Melanie said. "Rebecca, who attacked you and killed your brother?"

"Annabelle Alexandria."

"Peace be with! She did this?" President Oppenheimer asked.

"Of course, she didn't," Mr. Bancroft said. "Their cousin said the same thing, and I've already talked with King Mathias. He can confirm that Alexandria was in England at her guard post. She's very good at security, unlike this administration."

"He's lying!" Rebecca shouted. "She told me right to my face before she tried to stab me with the same knife that took my brother's life."

Silence engulfed the room as Melanie, Mr. Bancroft, and the president exchanged looks.

Rebecca was on the verge of breaking out of her chains.

"Look," the president said, "clearly someone attacked Rebecca and her sister. I don't feel they have done anything wrong. I say release them and let them return to school. Miss Evans, I want you to keep in touch with Rebecca. I also want security increased at Capitol Street."

"No way that's happening," Mr. Bancroft said. "That is a private school that I fund. I'll enlist my own security team. I can't trust you'll keep things in order."

The president seemed wary by this idea but nodded anyway. Melanie approached Rebecca, and, with a snap of her fingers, she broke the cuffs on Rebecca's wrists and ankles. "Come on, we'll go find your sister."

Rebecca stood and followed Melanie into a medical bay. A tired-looking, blonde-and-pink-haired girl sat on a table, and her face was swollen from crying. Rebecca quickened her pace to reach her sister.

Isabelle looked up and jumped down from the table, and the girls met halfway with a hug. "He's gone, Becky."

"I know," Rebecca said, now trying to stifle tears again.

"Why did she do that? Why are people mean?"

"I don't know, but I promise I won't let her do it again."

Isabelle stepped backward to look at her sister. "What do you mean by that? You won't kill her, will you?"

"No, what I meant was—" But Rebecca didn't know what she meant. Or did she truly want to kill Annabelle? It was what she had told Annabelle when she saw her. She had shouted those words as the woman had ran away on campus and before they had battled in the airport. Rebecca had promised Morgan and Andrew that she would kill the person who attacked her and Isabelle with the arrow incident. Perhaps Rebecca really wanted to do it.

"You girls okay?" Melanie asked when she caught up to them. "I know this has been a difficult time, but I'll have to take you both back to school now."

"What about Blake?" Rebecca asked. "Doesn't he get a burial?"

"I-I'm afraid not. It's a complicated procedure, given the circumstances, and I have no authority over that."

"But Blake deserves something! That's not fair to him or to us."

"I'm sorry, but he's now part of an investigation that may take months or years. I can't do anything about it."

With nothing left to say, the girls let Melanie drive them to Capitol Street. It was a long journey, but they had an escort. Melanie noted that the public had heard about what had happened. Between the police reports, the Saturn Society's opinion, and the mass media's spins on the stories, everyone had a different perspective on the situation.

It was likely people would try to hurt them, but Rebecca dared anyone to try. She no longer cared for anything except for Isabelle. Her only connection back home had been her godbrother, and now he was dead, and her mother would soon be too. The entire world could burn, and Rebecca would still do everything she could to protect her sister from harm.

Melanie pressed a button on the car just as they approached Washington DC. Isabelle asked her what it was for.

"Vibration waves. They interfere with magic. The more vibrations in the air, the more it hurts the user and disrupts whatever they try to do. Hopefully, nobody will try to attack us, but it's a standard precaution."

As they drove down Capitol Street toward the academy entrance, people lined the roadway, shouting and holding signs. The protesters surrounded them when they parked, and the agents in the escorting cars had to put a blockade around the car that contained the girls.

Melanie clipped the anti-mage device onto her, walked around to the back door and opened it.

Rebecca felt like she was back at the airport again when they had first arrived in America, except this time the people appeared more vicious. Their roar was as loud as the fans at any of her dad's soccer games. It echoed all around them. The atmosphere was daunting and unnerving.

As Rebecca and Isabelle exited the car, something landed at their feet and splattered onto them. Someone had thrown their drink, and now the sticky substance covered their shoes and pants.

"Arrest that moron!" Melanie said while pointing at a guy.

An officer advanced with a shield and knocked him to the ground.

But he wasn't the only one throwing things. More objects that wouldn't necessarily cause physical harm hit them.

Isabelle cried as Rebecca covered her, taking most of the mess to her backside.

Melanie pressed a button on the anti-mage device, and its red light turned off. She stretched her arms around them to stop objects coming nearby like a force field.

"It's okay, Issy," Rebecca whispered just as they were a foot from inside the gate.

Someone yelled very close from behind, and Rebecca turned to see a woman running right for them and tackled Rebecca to the ground.

Modern Physical Symbol

Chapter 12

Melanie pulled the woman off Rebecca just as soon as she had fallen on her. Melanie held the woman in her grasp and headbutted her. The woman was knocked out cold.

"Get inside," she shouted. "I'll close the gate."

The girls ran for it, and Melanie used magic to slam the metal bars shut. Protesters now surrounded her, all clambering to reach in and say their thoughts. Rebecca and Isabelle regarded the chaos with anxiety and fear. Rebecca couldn't understand how propaganda could so easily persuade people that two teenage girls posed a worldwide threat.

Rebecca looked at Isabelle, who was still wiping away tears. "Come on. I'll take you to your room." Rebecca tucked her sister under her arm.

Fortunately, nobody on the inside acted insane. But Rebecca didn't run across anyone on campus. Perhaps the administration had instructed them not to leave their dorms, or maybe they were all simply afraid.

Rebecca dropped Isabelle off at her dorm. To their surprise, Faith was not inside either, but her stuff was there.

"I think I'll take a shower," Isabelle said. "I feel icky."

Rebecca peered down the hallway. "You sure you're okay with being here alone?"

"Yes, of course. Faith is probably with some of her other friends. I'm sure she'll be back."

"Well, I don't know if Faith will still be as nice as she's always been, given what's happened."

"Faith trusts me. She won't be mean to me."

Rebecca wasn't one hundred percent sure about it, but she left Isabelle to her dorm room and went for hers. Upon arrival, she discovered someone had covered her and Morgan's dorm door with words like Spy, Criminal, Bitch, and Attention Whore.

She shook her head and entered. Morgan was not inside either. Where was everyone?

Rebecca went to close the door behind her, and someone pushed it back open. "I told you sluts to go away!"

A blur of red hair flew in and tackled Rebecca, who was ready to fight back, but no fists came for her.

Instead, Morgan gasped. "I'm so sorry! I thought you were Vanessa coming back to mess with our stuff. They keep writing things on the door, and now they're trying to find reasons to get you expelled so the school won't have to tolerate you." Morgan stood and extended her hand to help Rebecca up. "I just got out of class and was trying to get back here in time in case they decided to come this way. I just saw you walk in, and, well … I didn't expect it to be you."

"It's fine. No worries."

Rebecca searched for her journal. She had left it in her dorm, hidden away, during the break. She hadn't written in it much. Most of it was about Alvin and Lucy recently, but now she wanted to express her thoughts about what had happened with Blake. She found it and skimmed the pages to ensure no one had torn out any pages.

The door opened, and Andrew entered. "Becca! I didn't think you'd return after what happened."

"What did happen anyway?" Morgan asked. "The news has been saying all kinds of stuff. It's hard to believe any of it."

"Well … Sit down, and I'll explain."

She told Morgan and Andrew everything, from Annabelle's attack where she told Rebecca she had been after her all year, to the hard part— recounting Blake's death.

Morgan gasped, and Andrew lowered his head.

Rebecca further rehashed the interrogation from Mr. Bancroft, Melanie Evans, and the president.

Morgan nearly choked that she had met the president. "That's like, the coolest thing, to meet Oppenheimer. Sucks it was under those circumstances."

"We all know Oppenheimer is on Rebecca's side, but I'm more concerned about Victor Bancroft being there," Andrew noted.

"That's Vanessa's dad, right?" Rebecca asked.

"Yep," Morgan said. "That sack of cow crap has ordered an entire private security team to campus and checked us all when we arrived. Of course, Vanessa entered without any issues."

"Are they just ignoring the peace laws England broke with Annabelle being here?" Andrew asked.

"Bancroft said Mathias had confirmed Annabelle was with him. They believed it."

"That's interesting that Bancroft is in close talks with Mathias."

"He does handle foreign affairs, so it's natural that he does," Morgan said.

Both Rebecca and Andrew stared at Morgan with a quizzical look.

"What? My parents love talking American government and politics. Just because I got an agricultural scholarship doesn't mean I don't know other stuff."

*****

The talk of Annabelle's attack was far from over for Rebecca. Once again, people whispered about her in the hallways and turned their heads when she passed. It was as though she had caused Blake's death—which, according to most students, border patrol had killed him trying to sneak into the country. It was wrong and unfair that she had to bear listening to people falsify his death.

The classes proved no easier, especially those with Vanessa. She and her friends joked how they wished it had been Rebecca who died, and that was one thing Rebecca probably agreed with. Sometimes, she wished she could have taken Blake's place in the grave or a body bag, whichever the government decided to put him in.

But it wasn't just Morgan and Andrew who were still on her side. Before algebra, Rebecca was getting a dose of Vanessa's words when Alvin approached her. Venessa and her friends kept quiet to listen.

"Hey, I heard about what happened," Alvin said. "I'm sorry about your brother."

"Thanks …" She wasn't keen on discussing it in front of Vanessa, who was still hanging around trying to grab every word she could.

"If you need someone to talk to, I have an open-door policy." Alvin took her hand and held it.

Rebecca had to catch her breath. "Thanks, but it's better if I don't talk about it."

"Well, maybe I can help you take your mind off it." Alvin froze for a moment and seemed lost for words as they stood there awkwardly. "I was wondering if you wanted to go get coffee with me sometime soon."

She could hear Vanessa behind her scowl, and she thought of nothing more than to reply, "Sure. I'd like that."

"Really?"

Rebecca nodded with a smile.

*****

Rebecca stood outside the biology classroom with Morgan and Andrew. They waited for the teacher to open the door, and out of nowhere, Rebecca felt arms wrap around her. It was Lucy.

"Oh, Becca. I can't believe it. Blake didn't deserve that. You didn't deserve that." She sobbed into Rebecca's shoulder. "Please tell me that Isabelle wasn't there to see that happen."

"She was."

"I hope that bitch Annabelle gets what's coming to her soon. This is madness." Lucy broke their hug and looked at Rebecca. "I'm so sorry about the way I've been treating you. And I'm sorry about the things I said on the bus. I really miss you."

"I'm sorry too. I've missed you as well."

"Can you two lovebirds knock it off?" Vanessa had just walked up. "I mean, haven't we all heard enough about this sob story already?"

Rebecca and Lucy both faced her, but the door to the biology classroom opened. Rebecca lunged for Vanessa until Lucy's arm came up in front of her gut.

Vanessa walked by them, and it took a moment for Rebecca to cool down.

Rebecca turned to Lucy, and they hugged once more. Having Lucy back as a friend again made Rebecca feel less alone. She knew Lucy understood how important Blake was to her.

Nothing interesting happened for most of the week until magiology class. Rebecca was gathering her things with Morgan after class when Miss Stetson approached her.

"I need to speak to you in private. Now."

Morgan quickened her pace in packing and hurried from the classroom.

Rebecca and Miss Stetson were alone, and it suddenly hit Rebecca what Blake had said before he died. "Talk … to … Stetson."

"Blake could have been saved if you had learned magic sooner," Miss Stetson said.

"You weren't exactly helping me. He told me to talk to you. Why?"

Miss Stetson said nothing as she pulled a letter from her pocket and handed it to Rebecca.

Neveah,

I'm writing this letter to you instead of calling or emailing because I don't want this to get intercepted. Also, I don't know your number or email. It's been a while since we've spoken or seen each other. As I'm sure you know, England has a new king, and I don't think things will go in my favor with the way he talks. I'm afraid of what he'll do to me and my family. He'll come for all of us because of what I did.

When I helped, you told me you would be in debt to me, and, even though we've parted ways on bad terms, I hope you would still repay that debt.

I need you to teach Rebecca everything you know about magic. I will be sending her and her sister, Isabelle, to live with a relative of mine in New York, but I intend to enroll them in Capitol Street Academy, which I know is where you work now.

You and I were the best in dueling, but I still cannot reveal that I can perform such things. You, however, have made a name for yourself at the school in magic, and I want the best to teach Rebecca. I have no doubt Rebecca will have to protect Isabelle from Mathias. It's hard to explain.

Please do not write back. England will surely search the letter if it's addressed to me or anyone in my family. I must believe you will accept this as payment and hope you will teach her to the best of your abilities.

Best,

Sparrow

P.S. She still doesn't know, and I'd like to keep it that way.

Rebecca read it another time to ensure she comprehended everything her father had written. It was most certainly her father, but why did he sign off as Sparrow? She had even more questions, and she regarded Miss Stetson for the answers.

"You were supposed to teach me all this time? Half the school year is over, and I haven't learned a damn thing from you!"

"Watch your tone."

"No! Blake is dead because you didn't teach me anything. I could have saved him. I could have dealt with Annabelle and killed her myself."

"That is one of two reasons why I haven't taught you anything. Killing people is not what magic is for. I could tell by the way you have acted toward Vanessa that you would be very violent with magic. I've also seen your records at Sixsprings Academy. You and Lucy are troublemakers."

"We defended ourselves against bullies like Vanessa!"
"The point still stands, and, even now, I'm not so sure I should continue to teach you."

"What's the other reason? There better be a good bloody reason Blake is dead right now."

Miss Stetson waved her hand and pulled up a chair to sit in. She seemed slow to move, like her thoughts weighed her down. "I had intentions to teach you as soon as you got your mid-year report. I was purposely failing you and being hard on you, because that's what Capitol Street wanted. If they saw you were doing good, they would have been afraid that I was helping your father."

"That still doesn't explain why you couldn't teach me in private."

"Private lessons are only used for when a student is failing by mid-year reports. My plans were to hold these private lessons with you when you got back, because, by law, I would have to, and the school couldn't stop me."

Rebecca paced for a moment before finding a chair to sit in and pondered what Miss Stetson had just told her. The entire time, she had falsely hated Rebecca to please the Bancrofts, but Rebecca still didn't understand why she had to be the one to teach her.

"Why did my father keep it a secret that he knew magic?"

"Well, it's illegal in England. He came to America after being let go from soccer because he wanted to keep doing something competitive. He found me, and I taught him everything I knew, and then he learned more. He was a fast learner, and, while he was here pretending to be an assistant coach, he was actually illegally battling other magicians in secret."

"So, my father lied to me, my mother, and everyone else about what he was doing?"

"He never wanted to stop being competitive, and dungeon gladius has very few rules. He could keep going even with his leg injury; although he was stupid to do that."

Rebecca couldn't believe it. Her father had been living an alternate life—a criminal life—and he had lied about it. Rebecca wondered how much of their fortune was made from it. Instead of finding a job closer to home, he decided to keep abandoning Rebecca to live out his own fantasy.

"Why did he call himself Sparrow in the letter?"

"That was his persona while fighting to keep his identity secret. I was the Black Tempest."

"And what did he do to put you in his debt, and what went wrong between you two? And what is being kept a secret in the postscript part?"

"Is that really important to you?" Miss Stetson stood, approached the classroom door, and opened it, signaling that their conversation was over. "Starting tomorrow evening, you will begin these remedial lessons, if you hope to skid by this class. Come straight here after your final class period every day."

Rebecca stood and slowly walked out. She wanted Miss Stetson to say more, but she knew she wouldn't get anything else from her. Rebecca left without saying another word.

Modern Natural Symbol

Chapter 13

The worst of the winter dissipated as the snow melted from the grounds of Capitol Street Academy. A month had passed since Rebecca learned her true purpose for leaving home, but she was still struggling to grasp the use of magic.

Miss Stetson had put Rebecca through training five nights a week with at least three hours of intensive work. Miss Stetson had tried to drill into Rebecca that the key to being good at magic was to focus on what the magician wanted their magic to do. Rebecca had chosen the Physical-core path, as Miss Stetson called it the magic of warriors. It required a brain workout and lots of hot chocolate.

"Coffee and chocolate are great for replenishing your core," Miss Stetson explained. "There are also drugs that can give large but dangerous boosts to your abilities. Tobacco and marijuana weaken the core too but provide no benefits, which is why a lot of people don't have strong capabilities with their magic."

"Did you or my dad ever use them?" Rebecca asked.

"I did when I first started dueling seventeen years ago. I was desperate to win every match I could to make ends meet, but I was foolish. I suggest you do not make the same mistakes."

"What about my dad?" Rebecca asked again.

"Enough questions. Let's focus on breaking this table again."

Rebecca surveyed the oak table. Her task tonight was to snap a leg off it with a simple gesture by twisting her hand at it, similar to what Blake had done to the ladder lock at Kate's apartment. She stared at the leg and lifted her right arm and, like she was cranking a car with a key, gripped the air and turned her hand. A splint of wood popped out.

"You're not focusing hard enough."

"Yes, I am. It's just … hard."

"It's hard because you're letting it be hard. You don't have the confidence to do it. You automatically think you'll fail."

Rebecca raised her hand at the table leg again and twisted once more. Nothing happened. She gritted her teeth as she glared. She even imagined the leg to be Annabelle Alexandria's neck, but it didn't help.

Miss Stetson forced Rebecca's hand down. "Stop thinking about failure."

"I'm not!"

"Your father did the same thing when I was teaching him, and I did it too when I started out. I know you are. You still think Blake's death was your fault, but it's not."

"Yes, it is! I could have stopped her. I could have told Blake goodbye from the car, and we never would have gone into the airport where she was waiting. I could have been better at gladius if I had trained harder."

Miss Stetson faced the table, and, with a fist slam into the air, the entire table split in half. "Living with false failure and regret will never get you to this point. When you learn that, you will learn magic. Dismissed."

Rebecca had nothing more to say to Miss Stetson. She wondered though what her father thought he had failed at. She was too angry with Miss Stetson to ask, so she collected her things and left without saying another word.

******

Rebecca had told Morgan, Andrew, and Lucy about her private lessons, but she didn't tell them about the letter her father had written. While she trusted them, Miss Stetson told her it was best to have as few people know as possible to keep from being discovered.

146

Morgan suggested she should have taken the Natural-core path, as it was overlooked in battles, but, to the most trustworthy Natural warrior, every animal, plant, and even the weather would be willing to fight for her. Rebecca, however, didn't like the idea of innocent animals fighting battles at her command.

Andrew believed Spiritual would have been a better suit. Rebecca could speak to Blake and get advice from dead warriors, but she was afraid she would be stuck talking to Blake for the rest of her life and may not ever care to live on.

Lucy had another suggestion, and it was the most interesting one. She told Rebecca she should have pursued the Mental core.

"What is that?" Rebecca asked before entering magiology.

"I have no idea, but it's mentioned in our textbook, and we never talked about it in class."

"Wait. You actually opened and read your textbook?"

"Well, while you were still pissed off with me, I figured I had to at least try."

"I'm proud of you," Rebecca said with a smile.
Lucy blushed and smiled back.

As they took their seats, Miss Stetson entered and spread her arms in front of her. All the tables pushed away from them, and anyone who was sitting had fallen to the floor as their chairs slung from beneath them.

"From this point forward, we will be getting practical in class. For those of you who are going forth in one of the three cores, you will be focusing only on it and nothing else."

Lucy raised her hand "Miss Stetson …"

"What is it?"

"You said three, but, in our books, it says four."

"Are you referring to the Mental core?"

Lucy nodded.

"Then, if you had read further, you would have noticed that is not a real core but a myth."

"What makes it so?" Regan asked.

Rebecca scanned the room as whispers echoed. It seemed everyone had been interested in this core. Each student, including Vanessa and her gang, regarded Miss Stetson with wonder.

"I thought Dr. Robertson would have reviewed this in your history classes but very well then. It is rumored that before we had the ability to use magic, it only rested in the hands of the Peace Queen and her equal, the War King. Sometime after our ancestors signed the Peace Treaty, their powers left them and were dispersed into the rest of us."

"So only they could use the Mental core?" Morgan asked.

"Not just that, but they could control the other three cores. They possessed all of them and perhaps more."

"What does the Mental core do?" Lucy asked.

"The rumor is that it allows the person to read minds, control them, and even make the possessed see different images inside their head. You could even change a person's entire personality with it, if you're experienced."

More murmurs and whispers filled the room, but she was quick to silence them.

"As I said, this core is a myth. The only two people it had ever been tied to is the Peace Queen and the War King. No concrete evidence exists that it ever resided inside a normal human being. Now, let's resume finding your path in one of the three real cores."

After class, Rebecca's friends flanked her, all still scrutinizing their lesson. Morgan had learned how to do more with her already growing Natural core talent. She had made a miniature cloud form in her hand and contorted it into shapes. Andrew was the only student to choose the Spiritual core. According to Miss Stetson, he was just the twelfth to do so in Capitol Street's one-hundred-year history.

Lucy chose the Physical core despite trying to figure out the Mental core. "I think it exists. Why else would they print it in a schoolbook?"

"Stetson was right though," Andrew said. "Only the Peace Queen and War King have ever had possession of it, and that's still a rumor."

"Why do you want to read people's minds so badly?" Morgan asked.

"For plenty of reasons. You could become a detective or a judge and find out if someone's lying. You could find all sorts of evidence in someone's mind. And how cool would it be to know if your crush likes you or not? Then you won't have to dwell on it forever."

"Yeah. I see your point," Morgan said as she looked dreamily into the distance.

"Or you could just ask your crush," Rebecca suggested. She was quite frustrated with her own failures at magic that she didn't want to discuss it any further. It was all anyone wanted to talk about.

Alvin approached them from around the corner and stopped Rebecca and her friends. He looked flustered and spoke really fast. "Hey, Becca. So, I was wondering if you wanted to meet up this Saturday at the coffee shop across the street from campus?"

Rebecca felt her face redden as Morgan smirked at her. Andrew awkwardly scratched the back of his neck, and Lucy looked annoyed as she crossed her arms.

Rebecca looked back to Alvin. "Sure. I'll come."

"Great! I'll see you then." Alvin turned and walked away just as fast as he spoke.

*****

Saturday approached fast, and Rebecca had been grateful for that. Alvin's suggestion about hanging out a month ago kept getting put off because of her remedial magiology lessons. Rebecca never explained her situation to Alvin, and she didn't want to. She was afraid he would be too worried about her.

Morgan was so stoked to hear about the date that she asked Andrew to go to the coffee shop as well, but Andrew got the impression that they would be hanging out with Rebecca and Alvin. It took a lot of convincing from Morgan, because he wanted to study for finals, but he eventually came through.

Lucy was the only one who didn't like the idea of Rebecca hanging out with Alvin, and Rebecca didn't understand why. They and Morgan all hung out in their dorm together beforehand. Morgan fixed Rebecca's hair into a stylish ponytail. In all honesty, Rebecca didn't like ponytails, but Morgan was having too much fun, and Rebecca didn't want to stop her.

"I'm just saying," Lucy said, "he comes across a bit untrustworthy. Isn't he a politician in training? Politicians lie."

"It's just a date," Rebecca said. "I need a distraction from everything that's happened."

"But why him? He doesn't even seem like your type."

"Oh, come on, Luce," Morgan said. "Alvin isn't a bad guy. He's just really friendly to everyone, and he likes helping people."

"If you say so."

Neither Morgan or Lucy had dropped their first impressions of each other, and occasionally Rebecca had to ensure their subtle jabs didn't go any further. Morgan didn't understand why Rebecca had decided to fix things with Lucy if she had been so hellbent on staying away from her at the beginning of the school year. Meanwhile, Lucy believed that Morgan hated her. "She thinks I'm trying to take all the attention you give from her," she had once said.

Rebecca felt they were both out of their minds and that they should just drop their first encounter all together.

Rebecca and Morgan told Lucy goodbye and headed for the coffee shop. When they arrived, Rebecca saw that Alvin was already there. Morgan left Rebecca to herself and found a booth on her own, and Rebecca scratched her right ear as she nervously approached her date.

"Hey," Alvin said, standing to greet her. "Wow. You look fantastic with your hair like that."

"Thanks." Rebecca smiled like she was a showman at a circus. She sat and looked at Alvin, who stared right back. Both of them grinned and laughed.

"Sorry," Alvin said. "I just thought your eyes were like ten times brighter now that I can see them without your hair in the way."

"Well, don't get used to it. I'm not a fan of it being pulled back. Makes me feel naked."

"Why'd you do it then?"

"Morgan."

"She seems to like dressing you up. First Halloween and now today."

Rebecca eyed Morgan who had just stood up because Andrew walked in. She made him sit down next to her, clearly trying to keep him from going to Rebecca and Alvin, as he had thought they would.

"She likes him, doesn't she?" Alvin asked Rebecca.

"I think so, but I think she's too afraid to admit it to him."

"That makes two people in this room who has been afraid to admit their likeness for someone."

Rebecca turned to face Alvin. "What do you mean?"

"Well …" Alvin rolled his fingers on the table. "I haven't actually admitted that I like you, despite everything."

"I don't think you had to."

"What about you? Do you like me?"

Rebecca stared at Alvin then looked down. "Er, I'm not really sure how to answer that. I mean, I think you're a great guy. It's just … it's too soon for me to do this."

"Oh, yes. Sorry," Alvin said, scratching his neck.

"No, really. It's me who should be sorry. Actually, I need to use the loo." Rebecca stood and headed for the ladies room. She felt like she might burn up inside as she closed the stall door behind her.

There was no future with Alvin, she thought. Rebecca had no intentions of staying in America. She hoped that once she learned enough magic from Miss Stetson, she could go home and fight. At the same time, Alvin had every intention to stay in his home country, and she didn't quite understand why he thought this would work out between them. Perhaps he really was that deeply invested in her that he hadn't got that far. Maybe Rebecca was just a short run for him, or perhaps he simply wasn't interested in her in the way she had initially thought.

She needed to end it with him. Lucy might have been right. Maybe he wasn't her type. She took a deep breath and reached for the stall door handle to exit.

The bathroom door banged open, and Rebecca heard two sets of shoes pad across the floor, and two voices exchanged words. Rebecca stepped back from the stall door as she recognized the small voice as Cassandra and the shrilly one as Sheila.

"So, it was Edward who called for the Peace Queen? But didn't England start the whole war back then anyway?" Cassandra asked.

"Yes. They're such hypocrites. And now look at them having a war between each other because the treaty won't let them fight others. Morons," Sheila said.

"Okay, so Lord Edward was the first to call for it. And he ruled for … oh!"

The girls stopped talking, and Rebecca heard a strange silence with suckling sounds. She was certain they were kissing. She felt gross to listen to it too, but, at the same time, it stunned and now intrigued her. It lasted for a few moments before Rebecca heard them break it up.

"I wish we could do this more," Cassandra said.

"You know we can't. Imagine what would happen if anyone from the Society found out."

"The only person we're around is Vanessa. I don't think she would turn us in."

"Are you crazy? Nobody, not even she, would tolerate this. No. We're not risking our families' reputation for ourselves. Look at what they did to the Blacks."

"Screw them," Cassandra demanded. "Screw them and their backward ways. We deserve to be happy without their input."

Rebecca heard a smack, and then Cassandra groaned.

"We will not abandon the Society," Sheila retorted.

The door opened again, and Rebecca didn't need to guess who it was.

"Come on. What's taking you two so long? Did a troll walk in and try to kill you? I'm already stressed out from my failed magiology test. It's so unfair that bitch, Rebecca, gets special lessons, and I don't, and my father pays Stetson's salary."

"Sorry, Ness," Sheila said uncomfortably.

A second of silence passed before Vanessa spoke again. "Why is your face red, Cass?"

"Uhm, I did something wrong with my makeup, I think."

"Well, come on. I need you to tell me all the stuff about this history exam. Hmm, Becca the Bitch sounds like a pretty good nickname for that slut. Have you seen her whoring around with Alvin and that other girl from England?"

Vanessa's voice and their footsteps trailed off just as soon as the door shut. Rebecca quickly barged from the stall and hurried to leave the bathroom before Alvin felt that she had abandoned him.

Alvin, however, was standing when Rebecca returned. He looked like he was leaving.

Rebecca smiled. "Hey, I'm back."

"Hey, I'm sorry about what I said earlier, but I do have to leave. I've got an essay to write and two speeches to prepare."

"Oh ... well, okay then."

They both stood awkwardly for a moment before Alvin said goodbye and left Rebecca alone. She spied Morgan and Andrew who seemed to be having a good time together. She thought of joining them, but she didn't want to ruin their time. Then Lucy came to her mind and how she was probably feeling alone right now as well.

Perhaps she would go find her and have a proper bonding time with her. Rebecca missed the days of her and Lucy walking to her friend's home after school and having their fun talks and dreaming about what they wanted with their future. Rebecca would always say she and Isabelle would open a bakery together. Lucy never had a plan, but she said she wanted to be wherever Rebecca was. How poetic that they ended up at Capitol Street together.

As Rebecca exited the coffee shop, she no longer smelled coffee beans and vanilla. Her nose was introduced to something burning. Across the road, a plume of smoke rose from campus. Rebecca hurried to see what was happening. The closer she got, the more she could smell the smoky air. Crowds gathered around the performing arts building where firefighters were already on the scene with police, holding back the students.

It hit Rebecca so suddenly as pieces broke off the building and crashed to the ground. The dance hall was inside the building, and Isabelle had dance lessons today.

Without hesitating, Rebecca pushed through the crowd and even knocked down a few people. She reached the front where barriers were keeping everyone back, but Rebecca ducked underneath and bolted for the front doors. People screamed at her, and police ordered her to come back.

Rebecca entered the building despite all the imminent dangers. It was dark and smoky, and the only lights she could see were the exit and fire extinguisher signs.

"Damn it," Rebecca said under her breath. There was hardly any way to see, but she heard the doors open behind her. It was probably a firefighter trying to get her to come back out, but Rebecca quickly fell into the smoke and soldiered on. She wasn't letting anyone stop her from finding her sister.

She kept to the right side of the hallway to ensure she wouldn't get turned around. The deeper she went, the darker it got. Finally, she reached the dance hall, but debris blocked the door. The ceiling above it had collapsed. Rebecca had to move it.

She grabbed onto a piece of rebar protruding from a large slab of concrete and pulled as hard as she could. It didn't move.

"Issy!" Rebecca shouted at the door. "Issy! Are you in there?"

"Help!"

"I'm coming! Hold on!" Rebecca tried to pull again, but she got the same result. She gritted her teeth and tried once more, but nothing happened. "Okay, Becca," she said to herself. "You can use your magic. Come on!"

She recalled the lessons with Miss Stetson and how to control her focus on what she wanted her magic to do. Rebecca closed her eyes and gripped the rebar once more. She would move this block. She would save her sister. She would not fail. Three … two … one …

The rebar moved toward her, and the concrete came with it. She moved it just enough to get the door to swing open, and someone flung their arms around her. It was Faith.

"Thank you so much!" she cried.

"Where's Issy?"

Faith turned to look behind her, and Rebecca saw Ryan helping Isabelle. Her leg had a long cut on it. Rebecca ran to help her.

"She's fine," Ryan grunted.

"Fine? That's not fine!" Rebecca scolded. She went to pick up Isabelle herself, but Ryan tried to stop her.

"I've got her. You need to show us the way out," Ryan argued.

"No. Give me my sister. Now!" Rebecca used her magic to push Ryan, sending him flying backward into the wall.

"You'll get us all killed!" Ryan yelled at her as he slowly stood and re-approached her.

"Guys, come on!" Faith called out.

Ryan hesitantly exited, and Rebecca, holding up Isabelle, followed them out. They felt a shake in the hallway, and the crack in the ceiling couldn't hold any more than it already was. It collapsed, separating the Warren sisters from everyone else.

"Rebecca! Are you two all right?" Faith called out from the other side.

"Keep going! We'll go out the other way," Rebecca shouted between the debris. She coughed violently as she sucked in the ashes. Isabelle was having even more difficulty standing. She was getting heavier to hold up too.

Rebecca scooped her sister into her arms as they walked down the other end of the hallway. She didn't know if there was an exit on this side of the building. Perhaps it would be worse; however, it seemed most of the damage was surrounding the dance hall location. The air got clearer as they got away but not by much.

Rebecca's legs gave way from Isabelle's weight. "Come on!" Rebecca told herself, renewing her vow not to let her sister die. She lifted Isabelle once more and huffed the rest of the way. While her magic helped her with extra strength, it wouldn't help in getting extra oxygen. She felt herself fading fast. The light ahead was turning black.

An exit sign was in sight, and Rebecca tried to quicken her pace. She hit the door handle, and it flew open. The bright sky, the crowd, and clean air enveloped them.

Rebecca fell to her knees and gently placed Isabelle down. She then laid beside her and closed her eyes, looking right at her sister, and the sound of people cheering faded.

Modern Spiritual Symbol

Chapter 14

Rebecca had woken to the sound of a television in the background. The soft bed she laid in made her think she was in her dorm bed, but this one was propped up a bit. She opened her eyes to see white machines, white walls, and white tiled flooring surrounding her, and her bed featured fall-proof rails. She was in a place she hated more than anything—the hospital.

She then noticed tubes attached to her nose and an IV stuck in her wrist. She wanted to yank them out, but she figured they must be there for a good reason. All she could think about was finding Isabelle as soon as possible. Instead, she laid still and focused on the TV, which had an image of a burning building.

The news reporter chimed in. "Earlier today, firefighters were dispatched to Capitol Street Academy in Washington DC for a burning building. At around two o'clock, first responders tried to keep the crowd under control but were unable to prevent seventeen-year-old English native Rebecca Warren from running into the building. About twenty minutes later, two students who had been trapped in their classroom emerged from the building. On the other side, Warren exited carrying her sister. Both collapsed to the ground and are being treated at an undisclosed location for smoke inhalation and Warren's sister, a leg injury. The Warren sisters are refugees from England and have received a lot of negative backlash from some politicians, particularly the Saturn Society. However, many students on campus are calling Rebecca a hero. Investigators are unsure how the fire started but believe it is linked to arson."

A hero? Did Rebecca hear that right? She wondered who had called her that. Perhaps it was Faith, or maybe they got Morgan, Andrew, or Lucy to speak to the reporters. She found it difficult to think anyone else would say it like that.

The door opened as a nurse and a familiar face entered. Melanie Evans stood back as the nurse approached Rebecca. She perused her vitals and seemed to have found nothing of concern, because she immediately left Rebecca and Melanie alone in the room.

"I have to ask. Did you start the fire?" Melanie started.

"No!"

"I know you didn't, but it's good to have it on record." Melanie eyed the TV. "But someone definitely did."

"Do you think it was Annabelle Alexandria?"

"Since I have no evidence or witnesses, I cannot say that I think she did."

"And if you weren't investigating, who do you think did it?"

"Annabelle Alexandria. But I don't have the authority to bring her in for questioning, considering we've been told again that she's still in England."

Rebecca sat upright. Eager to get out of bed. "Where's my sister?" Melanie approached her and made her lie back down.

"You'll see her in just a few. Now, you said Alexandria had kidnapped your sister, attacked you and killed Blake, and then it so happens that a fire starts just above the classroom door where your sister is. Someone with a bow and arrow also attacked you two on campus earlier this year, which they identified the weapon as being made in England."

"What's your point? I know my sister and I have a big target on us."

"My point is that whoever started that fire is certainly trying to kill or seriously harm you and your sister. That person is from England, and the only people who want you from there is King Mathias. Alexandria also trained in archery, according to her arrest records before he expunged them."

"You know it's her, so get her before she kills one of us!" Rebecca's reaction seemed to surprise Melanie, but Rebecca didn't care. She was tired of the politics and bureaucracy waiting to decide who was guilty. Rebecca wouldn't wait much longer herself. "Start a war with him and dethrone him so me and my sister and other people can return home."

"Do you really believe that violence solves anything?"

"It stopped a lot of my bullies back home."

"And your school records show that once you started fighting, you were sent to the principal's office more often."

"The reports also doesn't show that I fought so much afterward because they messed with my sister."

"Maybe that's the problem then. You care too much that you let it scramble your mind. You don't think about the consequences. If you kill Alexandria, do you not think Mathias won't send another person?"

Rebecca fumed. She was about to press the call button for the nurse to come and remove Melanie from the room. She was tired of the way justice was done. She didn't care if society had been doing things a certain way for so long. Perhaps that's why these things were happening. For over seven hundred years, the world tried to cling onto their peace treaty, and they would look the other way to keep everyone happy while others suffered.

Melanie sighed. "You can see your sister now. I'll take you to her."

She wheelchaired Rebecca to another room where Isabelle slept with air tubes of her own attached to her nose and multiple bandages patching her leg.

Rebecca looked up at Melanie. "Will she be okay?"

"The doctor said she should be. I don't think she got anything worse than smoke and a cut."

"Can you leave us alone for a while?"

Melanie nodded and exited the room. It was now peace and quiet. The only thing Rebecca could hear was Isabelle's breathing. She felt terrible for her. Of all the people who could be deemed as a threat to the world, Isabelle should have never made that list. She was so innocent that she wouldn't harm a butterfly or even a spider.

Isabelle tossed and turned, and Rebecca stood from her wheelchair and crawled into bed with her. She knew Isabelle had endured too much already. A bad dream wasn't about to ruin her sleep. Rebecca wrapped her arms firmly around her and made shushing sounds as Isabelle whimpered. It took some time to comfort her, but Isabelle was finally over the nightmare and returned to her usual sleeping pattern.

This was a common thing for them for as long as Rebecca could remember. Nearly every night, Rebecca would be woken to Isabelle creeping into her bedroom to sleep with her. She wondered how Isabelle survived the night without her now that they had a completely different setup at Capitol Street. Perhaps Faith had assumed the role.

Once Rebecca felt that Isabelle was comfortable again, she too decided to drift off to sleep.

*****

A few days later, the doctors discharged Rebecca and Isabelle from the hospital. Melanie once again escorted the girls to school. This time, however, protestors were not there to greet them. Instead, Faith and other dance club members were waiting for them to arrive. Rebecca and Isabelle were met with applause and hugs. Faith's parents were there too, as well as Kate, Morgan, Andrew, Lucy, and Regan. Dr. Robertson and the dean had even attended to give Rebecca an award for her heroism.

Unfortunately, not everyone was as grateful. Ryan approached Rebecca when she, Morgan, Andrew, and Lucy were heading back to the hall to celebrate their well-being.

"You don't deserve this. You nearly got us all killed."

Lucy stepped between them "Get away from her, Ryan. You're just mad that you were the damsel in distress and she was the knight."

"I'm mad because she doesn't trust anyone with her sister."

"No, you're wrong," Rebecca said. "I trust her with my friends here, but not with you."

Rebecca and her group continued walking, leaving Ryan alone.

Miss Stetson was also not impressed with Rebecca's actions. When they met for the evening, she asked Rebecca to give a play-by-play description of the situation. Once Rebecca finished telling the story, Miss Stetson shook her head.

"You could have punched a hole in the wall or pushed all the debris out of your way and cleared a path. And using it on another student is normally an automatic ban from all campus clubs."

"Sorry I'm not living up to your expectations, but I was only concerned with saving my sister. Sheesh."

"You got lucky saving her, but what'll happen when Annabelle decides to show up again?"

"I'll kill her."

Miss Stetson laughed. "You? A killer? Do you really think you have the stomach to take someone's life? Take it from me. You don't want blood on your hands."

"Have you killed?"

"I won't disclose that with you."

There was a pause.

"Well, how am I supposed to break down walls to save people? My magic is limited."

"Your imagination is your limitation, and your emotions can hold you back too. A warrior thinks with her mind. Not her heart."

Rebecca had never thought she was one to be emotional. She didn't have much care for many people in her life, but, as she thought about the way she had acted during the fire, perhaps she had been too concerned with Isabelle at the time. Maybe if Ryan hadn't been acting so superior, Rebecca could have focused on punching a wall.

"I've said it before, and I'll say it again. You care too much for Isabelle. She'll be the death of you."

"Then she shall be. Nobody will harm my sister again so long as I live."

"Then I suggest you start training harder and with your mind, not your heart."

*****

Magic came easier to Rebecca. She could perform the basics more practically and without having to think about it. It was becoming second nature, but Miss Stetson noted she still had a long way to go before using it in true combat.

If only she could practice her abilities on Vanessa. She had thought about joining the magic section of dueling club, but Miss Stetson denied her access so that Vanessa wouldn't have her father investigate their remedial lessons.

Rebecca attempted to challenge her rival to a gladius duel, but she declined, claiming it was a waste of her time.

But what wasn't wasting her time was that Vanessa was still saying stuff about Rebecca behind her back. Not many people apart from Cassandra and Sheila cared to listen, though as many were still impressed with Rebecca's rescue.

During English, Mr. Wallace tried very hard to pretend that Vanessa wasn't magically throwing paper balls at the back of Rebecca's head.

"Miss Warren, would you please pick up the trash from around your desk before you leave?" he asked as she passed him on the way out the door.

"Why don't you do it? Aren't you the one who is always covering up for whatever mess Vanessa makes?"

Mr. Wallace tried to find words, but said nothing.
"And you can take all of my participation points for the day if you'd like."

Rebecca hurried to catch up with Morgan and Andrew, but she didn't know Vanessa was behind her until she heard her voice pretending to whisper very badly.

"I swear it's like she actually saved people who were worthy to be saved. I mean, what the hell can those dancing nerds do with their lives? Nobody needs that crap."

Rebecca looked at Andrew who shook his head at her.

"And then there's her sister, who is a complete waste of space. All she does is pretend everything is all kittens and rainbows."

Rebecca's breathing deepened, and Morgan elbowed her. If she was trying to distract her from Vanessa, it wasn't working.

"And then it's so funny how she manages to save those people but not her godbrother. Poor Blake is now a rotting corpse with a coroner's hand up his ass, and it's all her fault."

Rebecca cracked her knuckles as she closed her hands into fists. She stopped walking and turned around on a dime. Vanessa and her friends had just turned down another hallway, laughing. Rebecca followed them.

The hallways were too crowded to catch up to her, but Rebecca had her eyes locked on the back of the girl's head. Vanessa had no idea, and she told Sheila and Cassandra to continue on while she stopped at the bathroom. Rebecca caught the door.

Just before Vanessa could open a stall door, Rebecca grabbed the back of her head and slammed it into the door. Vanessa shrieked and fell to the floor while holding her forehead. Rebecca stomped on the girl's back, and her forehead contacted the solid, cold, tiled flooring. Something red splattered from Vanessa's impact, and somehow, she was still half-conscious as she rolled onto her back. She was lucid just enough to see Rebecca sit on top of her and put her fists into Vanessa's face. Rebecca had so much fire in her eyes that she thought everything was darkening around her. All she wanted was to beat the life out of her and never stop—not until Vanessa was a puddle of blood.

Someone grabbed Rebecca from behind.

"Get off me!" she yelled, but they didn't stop coming for her. Rebecca retaliated, and more hands grabbed her and dragged her backward. She saw brunette and redheaded figures.

"Snap out of it, Becca!" Lucy ordered.

Rebecca felt a hard smack across her face. It took a moment, but Rebecca finally regained her composure and saw what she had done.

"Oh jeez, what do we do?" Morgan asked as they all stared at Vanessa's limp body; she was still breathing, but she was not moving. Rebecca surveyed her hands. Her knuckles were split from how hard and how much she had punched Vanessa. Rebecca inspected Vanessa's face, which was black, blue, and red.

"Get Becca out of here," Lucy said. "I'll deal with her."

"What are you going to do?" Morgan asked.

"Just get her to her dorm and clean her up and pretend you never saw this. Both of you."

Morgan nodded and went to pick Rebecca off the floor, and the two of them walked out, leaving Lucy to the scene.

Chapter 15

The dormitory was dead silent. So silent that Rebecca could hear her heart beating fast. The rate was so fast that the blood in her veins penetrated her brain like a sewing machine needle jackhammering a piece of clothing. Her mind was being stitched back together after unleashing all her rage on Vanessa.

Morgan and Andrew had brought Rebecca to the girls' room, where they waited to see what would come next. Rebecca could tell by the look on their faces that they feared her, especially Morgan. She had witnessed the attack firsthand. She told Andrew what had transpired, including what Lucy had instructed them to do.

Hours passed without anyone saying a single word. While Morgan and Andrew were in the background watching her, Rebecca fantasized about all the things she wished she had done, like ensure Vanessa could not get up from that bathroom floor alive or catching up to her and attacking in the hallway so everyone could see how much of a threat she really was to the world.

Whatever Lucy had planned, the longer it took, the more it made sense she would take the blame for what had happened. This was nothing new to Rebecca. Back home, before everything had changed, Lucy had always taken the fall for Rebecca's mistakes and battles she fought. Lucy would get into some of the worst trouble, and Rebecca would get to walk away from it. Why would this be any different today?

What made it different was that she didn't want Lucy to take the blame. Rebecca wanted the world to know she was no longer the person to mess with. It wasn't fair that Lucy would get the credit. It would be her that Mathias would fear, not Rebecca.

The doorknob twisted, and the door opened to reveal Lucy, her face and arms covered in bandages.

"What the heck happened to you?" Morgan asked.

"Got into a fight with Vanessa. At least, that's what everyone else thinks, but only the four of us know the real story." She waved her arm around and pointed at herself. "I did all of these cuts and bruises to myself with some of my own physical magic. Ended up knocking myself out, and a student found us both lying on the floor."

"So, you took the blame?" Andrew asked.

"Of course. And now me and Vanessa will receive a temporary suspension from classes and clubs, with daily detentions for the next three weeks."

"She's still alive?" Rebecca asked.

"Fortunately, yes or else I would have gone to jail for murder. Or maybe both of us would be dead. I think I'd rather kill myself than go to prison here."

"This is insane!" Morgan shouted as she jumped from the bed and pulled on her hair. "I mean, why take the blame?"

"Because if it was Rebecca, she and Isabelle would have a one-way ticket to Mathias. The Bancroft family has it out for Rebecca, and this was the perfect excuse to kick her out of the country—maybe even hand deliver her to the king."

"But not you?" Andrew pressed.

"This was my first time getting in trouble at Capitol Street, and, in this scenario, I was also knocked out. It's just as much Vanessa's fault as it is mine."

Silence filled the room again, but only for a moment. It was Andrew who had another question. "But didn't Vanessa tell someone that it was Rebecca?"

"She hasn't woken up yet. Not all the way, at least. She did try to blame Rebecca, but with the other student and me both saying I fought her, they are handling my story as the truth."

"Brilliant," Morgan said sarcastically and grabbed Rebecca's hand. "So tomorrow when Becca walks into class, they won't question why her knuckles are close to showing bone?"

"I have a solution for that, but I can only talk to Rebecca about it. I need you two to meet us in the commons after we're finished talking."

Morgan and Andrew exchanged glances and then looked to Rebecca.

She nodded toward them, and they left without another word. While Rebecca liked her friends, she was glad they were gone for a few minutes.

Lucy sat beside her. "I have to admit, what you did has me scared of and for you. I think after what I did for you, I am owed an explanation about what has gotten into you."

"I don't owe you anything. I didn't ask you to get in trouble for me." There was a moment of silence again, and Rebecca swallowed hard. "I'm sorry. I'm just so pent up since Blake died. All I want to do is go after Annabelle. I'm tired of waiting for her to come to me. I want to get my hands around her throat and just make her feel what I felt when she killed the only person who gave a shit about me."

"Hey," Lucy said as she took Rebecca's hand. "I care about you too." She pointed at the door. "And so do Morgan and Andrew. And Isabelle does probably more than anybody else, which is why you need to get yourself under control before she sees this side of you."

"I'm worried that what happened to Blake will happen to her too. I can't lose her. She's all I've got."

"I agree that Annabelle deserves everything you can think of doing to her, but you have to control yourself. Vanessa is trying to get under your skin, but she's not your threat."

Rebecca stood and faced Lucy. "Do you know the real reason why my parents sent me to America? To this school in particular?"

"Because it's the best place for an education, as all of their brochures kept telling us?"

Rebecca took a deep breath, knowing she was about to break a promise to Miss Stetson. She went into detail about how her father had written a letter to Miss Stetson, giving her instructions to teach Rebecca magic for battle. Rebecca even noted that Miss Stetson owed her father for something he had done for her and that she took her time to teach anything to her.

"If Miss Stetson hadn't slept on me, I could have stopped Annabelle right there, and Blake would be alive," Rebecca finished.

"I wonder why your dad never explained this to you before you left France. Then you could have annoyed her to teach you."

"Exactly! I swear he acts like he cares about me, but then he does things like this. I'm so sick of all my family's secrets."

"Well, I'm sure your dad had a good reason for not telling you about Miss Stetson. I feel like my dad left me and Mum for a good reason, but that still doesn't change the fact that I want to strangle him if I ever met him."

"I hate our dads."

"So, back to today's situation … There's still one more thing for you to do in order for this plan to work."

Lucy found Morgan's TV remote and turned on the television and switched it to the government channel. Some state senator from Delaware was standing and talking to a bunch of bored politicians. In the background, Rebecca noticed Victor Bancroft looking at his phone, and his thumbs were twiddling fast.

"He can't leave until that guy stops talking," Lucy said, "but when he does, he's coming straight here to ask you questions about what happened. We can't let him do that."

"But he runs this school, and how can I hide my hands?"

"Follow me."

The girls left the room and walked down the hallway toward the stairs.

"You need to be in a state where he can't talk to you," Lucy said.

"And what do you have in mind?"

They stopped at the landing.

"You need to end up in the infirmary along with Vanessa and knocked out cold so you can't talk."

"I'm sorry, but I won't hurt myself. I don't have the guts to do what you did to yourself."

Lucy took a deep breath. "I know you won't. That's why I'm going to do it."

Lucy grabbed Rebecca's shoulders and spun her to face the steep stairwell. With a shove, Rebecca was falling. She screamed as her knees cracked on the steps, followed by a crunching sound from her hands. With a hard thud to the forehead on the landing, Rebecca was out.

*****

Rebecca woke to a sunset blinding her eyes from the window nearby. She was laying on a soft bed and pillow, and other beds surrounded her as well, with curtains covering some of them. Rebecca tried to move, only to find her arms were stuck in place with one of them in a cast and one of her legs was suspended with the same material.

Suddenly, the doors down the hallway barged open, and Rebecca shut her eyes.

"This is an outrage!"

Rebecca's ears perked up, but she didn't dare look again as she laid still.

Mr. Bancroft was raging at the school nurse. "My daughter! My own daughter was nearly killed, and you let that girl walk away?"

"Both of them were in rough shape," the nurse said. "I'm not sure who did more damage to the other. Both used magic, which is illegal outside of dueling club."

"But you let her go! Did you even inform the police or my security? What in the hell do I even pay you for? I'll make sure my money no longer goes to your department after this incident!"

There was a moment of silence apart from footsteps and someone shifting around. Rebecca wondered if Mr. Bancroft was kneeled beside Vanessa. She assumed the girl wasn't too far away from her.

"I know you're awake, Warren!"

A hand grabbed her shirt collar, and she opened her eyes out of shock. She was staring face to face with Mr. Bancroft. His breath smelled like pork, and his eyes were filled with little blood vessels ready to pop. His hand let go immediately as an invisible force pulled him away.

"That's enough, Victor." It was Miss Stetson. Rebecca figured she had been in the room the entire time.

"Don't you dare you use your magic on me, Neveah. I'll put a stop to that very fast."

"I was asked to be here to keep things civil."

Mr. Bancroft approached Rebecca again.

She tried to play it off as though she had no idea what was happening.

"So how did you end up here, if you had nothing to do with Vanessa's injuries?" he asked her.

"She had fallen down the steps coming out of her room," the nurse interjected. "A few people were there to see it."

"But these scars on her knuckles ..." Bancroft grabbed Rebecca's hand. "They indicate that she has been in a fight."

"Those more likely came from falling. I'm sure you see the rest of her body isn't in great shape either."

Rebecca wondered what her face looked like, but she didn't see a mirror. She couldn't believe Lucy thought this was the best plan, but, when Rebecca tried to think of other ideas, perhaps she had the only plan.

"So where is this other girl?" Bancroft asked. "Who is she?"

"Lucy Ferguson," Miss Stetson said.

"That's the other girl from England? I told the president they were bad news, and this is exactly what I was warning him against. Oh, there will be hell for this one. And I know that Warren has something to do with it, and I'll prove it."

"You should leave now before I call security," the nurse said.

Bancroft snickered. "Do you think my security team will come and stop me?"

But Bancroft didn't bother to wait to have that question answered. He exited the room, and the nurse followed him, but Miss Stetson stayed behind.

She looked at Rebecca and said in a low voice, "You should be ashamed for this mess."

Rebecca said nothing, and Miss Stetson walked away. Rebecca peered at Vanessa, who was laying opposite of her. It was a wonder she was still at the school and not in an actual hospital. She had a machine nearby feeding tubes to her. For just a moment, Rebecca felt bad about what she had done.

She found a mirror on her bedside table and picked it up to look at the monster she was slowly becoming.

Capitol Street Academy

T. Russell Parker

Chapter 16

Vanessa had not returned to classes for several weeks. The first week, she was cooped up in the infirmary, and for the next two, she served her detentions. It was the most peace Rebecca had received while at Capitol Street Academy since her first day. Not even Sheila and Cassandra were saying things about her. They seemed lost without their leader, but Rebecca had noticed they had become more open with their fling without Vanessa's presence.

When Vanessa did return, she still did not say a word against Rebecca. It made her wonder if her bully had finally given up on provoking her.

Lucy, however, was still in detention when Vanessa returned. Mr. Bancroft ensured she served a longer detention stretch. As unfair as it was, the punishment could have been much worse.

Rebecca shifted her focus to exams—or at least she tried. She decided to heed Lucy's warnings of becoming obsessed with Annabelle Alexandria and wanted to pass her classes in hopes of still being at Capitol Street next year in order to stay with Isabelle—assuming they were not going home by then.

Fortunately, she was best friends with the smartest kid in school. She and Morgan asked Andrew for help in their studies, to which he was happy to oblige. During those weeks that Vanessa and Lucy missed, Rebecca, Morgan, and Andrew met frequently in the commons to study. Usually, it resulted in Morgan getting bored, and so they would call it quits earlier than they planned.

Rebecca thought today would be no different, but, as she looked through a window into the commons, she noticed Andrew was alone, even though Morgan's things were still there.

Rebecca entered and greeted Andrew. "What's up, genius?"

"Oh, hey!" Andrew put down the book he'd had his nose in to look at Rebecca.

"So, biology today?"

"Yeah, but it looks like Morgan's gonna be late coming back. She's been away for a while now." Andrew seemed to be in deep thought, and it didn't seem like it was about studying.

Rebecca sat on the floor and placed her backpack to the side. "So, Andy, have you ever been on a date?"

He dropped his book and scrambled to pick it up. "No, of course, I haven't. Do you think I care about that kind of stuff? It's a waste of time." He reopened his book, but Rebecca doubted it was on the correct page; he was simply gazing at the field of words.

"Come on, you can't think of one girl you'd like to date? Or guy? I'm not judging."

"Guy, girl, alien. I have no interest in relationships. They just get in the way of success."

"So, you don't even have a desire to have kids and give them a chance to have success too?"

Andrew closed his book and surveyed the cover. "My father wanted me to have success. He was the only one who tried to help me get a good education, but, being the chief of our tribe, he had to pretend he hated me for my wishes. It pained him, and it hurt me too. My father couldn't be who he wanted to be—proud."

"Why did your tribe not want you to have an education?"

"Because that's not what Tahoes are. We are a nation who don't play by the rules of the civilized world. Civilized and Tahoe societies should never mix according to many in my society. It's why my people left this side of the continent and moved west. We saw what they had in store, and we would either have to accept it and become them or go elsewhere."

"Or you could have fought."

"At the time, England ruled this land, and the Peace Treaty protected them. We would have fallen. When America became its own country, we made a deal with them to leave us alone, and we would allow one of the peacelines claim rule over us so we could also be protected under the treaty."

"Who is your peaceline ruler?" Rebecca asked.

"No one knows. It was lost to history. Whoever it is, even they may not know. It's a large reason Tahoes don't leave our lands. It would be bad for us if that peaceline died. It would mean war. There are some like the Saturn Society who believe in American supremacy across North America. If they knew and were in power..."

While the history lesson was intriguing, Rebecca gave up on playing love doctor. She believed Morgan liked Andrew, but she had hoped the feeling would be mutual. Perhaps she was wrong, but Andrew's answer disappointed her.

"Well, I'm going to find Morgan and get her back here. You think she's in the dorm?"

"Probably," Andrew answered dryly as he picked at a silver ring on his finger.

Rebecca stood and climbed the same stairs she remembered falling from. The loud thuds from tumbling down made her head hurt just thinking about it. She was amazed she even survived it. She still occasionally got headaches, and her leg was still sore. They both had caused her to miss gladius training.

When Rebecca reached the landing and started down the hallway, she heard shouting from her room. It sounded like two people. Rebecca quickened her pace, thinking Vanessa was starting more trouble again. When she opened the door, she discovered Morgan and Lucy.

"You could have killed her!" Morgan spat.

"She's alive. She's right there," Lucy said, pointing at Rebecca.

"Becca, how come you didn't tell me you got shoved down the stairs by this twat?"

Rebecca had not told Morgan nor Andrew about what Lucy had done, but that was because she thought Lucy had already told them.

"There was no point in bringing it up," Rebecca said.

"There were many points to," Morgan said. "Did you even think about the possibility that you could have died or got injured to the point where you couldn't walk again?"

"I didn't really have a choice," Rebecca said. "Lucy surprised me with it."

"You bitch!" Morgan cried to Lucy. She charged toward her, but Rebecca got between them. She *pushed* them both back, and they fell onto Rebecca's and Morgan's beds.

"If you say a word about it, you'll get Rebecca in more trouble," Lucy said.

"It was the only way, Morgan," Rebecca said. The fiery redhead's anger slowly faded from her face.

"Fine, but did you know Isabelle came by to ask me what was happening with you? She's been worried sick about you, and it's not fair to her to have all of this going on."

"Which is exactly why we did it this way," Lucy said. "Otherwise, they both might be dead by now from Mathias."

"What's done is done, so drop it," Rebecca ordered.

Morgan huffed out of the room, leaving Rebecca and Lucy to themselves.

"Morgan did make a good point though," Lucy said. "I hope you stop all this nonsense, for your sister's sake."

"Let me worry about that."

Lucy turned and left the room too.

Rebecca now only had her thoughts to herself. She kept replaying the scene of Vanessa's mangled body and how she pictured it to be Annabelle Alexandria's. She knew her friends were warning her about ignoring the kidnapper, but they didn't know what it was like. They didn't see Blake die, his wound flowing with dark blood, and they didn't see the light leave his eyes. They didn't hear the laughter Annabelle echoed throughout the room.

And Rebecca never had a proper goodbye. The authorities had whisked her away immediately after his death and interrogated her as though it was all her fault. People still blamed her for all the bad things in this country and back home. People wanted her and her sister dead.

Rebecca sat at her desk, holding her head from all the pain her thoughts were causing, and fell asleep.

Rebecca was now back home, playing hide and seek with her sister in the backyard. Rebecca was searching for Isabelle and found her behind a large rock—her usual hiding place.

"Got you!" Rebecca yelled out.

Isabelle giggled. "Okay, now I'm goin' to hide again. Close your eyes and count to ten!"
Rebecca did as she was told and started counting. Most kids would swap roles in hide
and seek, but Isabelle never wanted to seek because she was afraid of losing Rebecca
forever. It also didn't help that Rebecca was far better at hiding. She knew where her
sister always hid, but Rebecca was good at elongating it to make it look as though it was
difficult.

"Ten! Ready or not, here I come!" Rebecca called out. She slowly walked
around to look for her. She knew Isabelle was hiding behind the large oak tree with the
treehouse, but Rebecca searched in other places first.

The back door opened to the large house she called home. Rebecca looked and
saw that it was her brother, Ray.

"Hey, butthead. What are you doing?" he asked as he approached her.

"Go away! I'm playing with Isabelle. Something you never do."

"I do too! You're just never around to see it."

"Liar."

"Ask her then. Where is she anyway? I thought you said you were playing with
her?"

"It's called hide and seek, idiot." Rebecca quickened her pace and headed to the
oak tree.

Ray followed her.

"Got you!" Rebecca said as she jumped around it, but no one was there.

"Wow, you're terrible," Ray said.

"Shut up! She should be here," she said, panicking. "She always hides here
after the rock."

"Maybe she tricked you this time?" To Rebecca's surprise, he looked worried
too.

"You know that's not like her." She clapped her hands together and yelled,
"Issy! Where are you?"

But no matter how many times Rebecca yelled for her sister in the yard, she heard nothing.

"Issy! Where are you?"

Morgan's voice pulled Rebecca from her desk. She was no longer looking at her backyard but instead a computer screen and books. She was back in her room at Capitol Street.

"Are you okay?" Morgan asked.

Rebecca didn't answer. She was trying to catch her breath. The dream she had experienced was something real, something that did happen. It was something she wanted to forget, and she was grateful Morgan had woken her. She pulled her friend in for a hug.

"Everything is fine," Morgan said as she patted Rebecca's back.

"I'm sorry you saw me like that."

"You don't have any head trauma from the stairs, do you?"

"I don't know. I haven't thought about that memory in years."

"Do you want to talk about it?"

Rebecca broke her hug from Morgan. "No."

"Are you sure? It might make things better if—"

"I said no!"

Morgan backed away.

"I'm sorry. I just— I can't talk about that memory. It's best to be forgotten."

"Sure thing. I won't bring it up again."

The computer dinged, and Rebecca turned her attention to it. She was relieved there was something to distract her from what had happened, but she wasn't too pleased when she saw it was an email from Alvin.

Hey, Becca,

I'm sorry about how our date went a while back, and I thought maybe things just weren't meant to be for us, so I decided to leave you alone, as that was what I thought you wanted. But, ever since the fire, I wanted to talk to you again, because I've been worried about you. Anyway, I was hoping we could meet up and hang out maybe tonight and go see a movie just on the west side of campus across the street. I don't know how much you like movies, but, if you'd like to, let me know as soon as possible.

Alvin

Sent from ePhone

Rebecca did not respond, as she wasn't sure about it. She still had some feelings for Alvin, but, after their first—and currently last—date, things didn't go well. As the email had said, they hadn't spoken since then.

"Becca, when do you think it's a good time to ask someone to be official?" Morgan inquired from her bed.

Rebecca was taken aback by this question. "Er, I guess you just have to know it's the right time, but you won't know it until you do."

"What does that even mean?"

"I don't know, but I've heard my mum tell Ray that once. Why do you ask?"

"Well ..." but Morgan never answered.

Rebecca turned around and looked at her. She was staring at her hands.

"If you like Andrew so much, why don't you ask him out?"

"Girls don't ask boys out. Not usually, at least. And we've been friends for over a year. I'm sure I'm stuck in the friend zone by this point."

Rebecca laughed. "Girls don't get stuck in the friend zone. And who cares what the norm is? Just go for it, and, if he says no, you two will still be great friends."

"How did you make it look so easy with Alvin?"

"I didn't. It just sort of happened fast. I never dated anyone before him, but I doubt it'll last."

"What makes you say that?"

"Well, you know we haven't spoken since the coffee shop. He wants to see a movie tonight, and I don't know if I should." Rebecca showed Morgan the email, who got all giddy about it.

"You should go! Free movie if it goes sour. You guys should try one more time."

"Fine, but you have to ask out Andrew before I get back."

Morgan paused to think about it. She reluctantly agreed, and Rebecca sent an email to Alvin, accepting his invitation.

Chapter 17

And so the plan was in motion. After a few email exchanges, Rebecca met Alvin by the water fountain in the central part of campus. It felt odd to be back here. The last time they were here, Annabelle Alexandria struck an arrow into Alvin's leg. Rebecca hoped they could make a new and not-so-gruesome memory. Still, she had made a detour to the dueling arena and snuck out a knife just in case trouble came along.

As Rebecca had entered, she noticed Regan was by herself, alone, and in tears. Rebecca didn't want to be seen coming in, but she abandoned her mission and proceeded to her gladius trainer.

"Oh, hey, Becca. I didn't see you there." She quickly wiped her tears.

"Hey, what's up? You all right?"

"No— I mean yes, I'm fine."

Rebecca sat beside her. "What's wrong?"

Regan took a deep breath. "My parents got fired from their jobs after Vanessa's father cut funding. He also filed a complaint saying they nearly killed her after she and Lucy got into their fight, so no other hospital that wants to keep a reputation will hire them. Now they're screwed out of a job, and I don't know if I'll be back here next year. If they can't afford it, I may not be able to pursue my goal as a professional gladius duelist."

Rebecca couldn't help but feel guilty for what had happened to Regan. Had Rebecca not beat up Vanessa, Regan's parents could still be working somewhere else. Now, her fate was up in the air.

"I'm so sorry, Regan."

"It's not your fault. I shouldn't have threatened to kick her out of the club."

"You shouldn't let people walk over you though. You stood up for integrity and honesty that day. I respect you for that, and I think, no matter if you come back next year or not, you'll find a team who'll accept you for those values alone. Plus, you're a badass anyway."

"Thanks," Regan beamed. "Was there something you came here for?"

"Er ..." Rebecca had no idea what to say.

Regan stood and pointed to a pile of swords. "Could you help me move these back to the locker rooms? Can't leave them out overnight."

"Sure thing."

As they grabbed the swords and headed to the lockers, Rebecca noticed an opened box with knives inside. Rebecca purposely dropped a sword nearby it. "Oops," she said at the loud crash. "I'll get it."

Regan put her swords on the racks of a locker.

Rebecca did the same but at a faster pace. When she reached the last sword on the floor, she swiped a knife from the box and placed it in her back pocket.

Regan never noticed when she closed all the boxes.

*****

The sun was close to setting when Alvin arrived and greeted Rebecca at the fountain. It was their first time speaking to each other since their coffee shop date. Alvin looked like a stud with his buttoned-up t-shirt and blue jeans, and Rebecca had on a dark blue blouse with light-colored jeans. While Alvin looked nice, he reminded Rebecca of the boys her age back home who would attend the parties her family went to. She didn't like those boys.

But no matter, Rebecca wanted to give Alvin another chance. She didn't feel like there was much at Capitol Street to make her happy and forget all the bad things that had transpired. Perhaps Alvin's movie date was a way to escape it. Rebecca also hoped Morgan would keep her end of their deal and ask out Andrew.

When Rebecca and Alvin arrived at the gate to leave, however, the guard stopped them. "You're not allowed to leave at this time of the day," he said to Rebecca.

"Why not?"

"Due to recent events, your off-campus pass has been stripped."

Rebecca noticed the guard wore a pin shaped like the planet Saturn and knew instantly who was behind this decision. She couldn't argue against him, so she and Alvin headed back up the path.

"This sucks!" Rebecca said.

"Yeah, but there is a solution to this."

"What is that? We sneak out?"

"Exactly! Come on. I know a spot we can get out that will put us just a few blocks from the theater."

"Are you sure about this?"

"Yeah. I did it all the time my freshman year."

Rebecca didn't question Alvin anymore, and they cut through a path in the campus woods to a part where the perimeter fence was badly damaged. As soon as they reached the sidewalk, Rebecca was stunned to see Isabelle out and about as well—and she was with Ryan Bostick.

"Issy, what are you doing out here?"

"Oh, hey, Becky! Ryan and I were going to the movies tonight."

Rebecca's and Ryan's gazes met. She hadn't forgotten the way he had acted during and after the fire, but Rebecca returned her attention to her sister. "You know how dangerous it is for you to be out here? You should have told me that you were coming here with him, so I could have kept an eye on you."

"Back off, Rebecca," Ryan said, stepping up. "She can make her own decisions, and she doesn't need you to watch over her."

"Shut up, Ryan," Alvin said. "This has nothing to do with you."

Ryan kept his mouth closed even though he seemed ready to open it again.

"Why do I have to tell you everything?" Isabelle asked. "You never tell me what you're doing."

"Issy, don't you remember what happened at the airport? That woman is still out there, and she's after us. You have to trust that I have good reasons for keeping a close eye on you."

"You know," Ryan started, "you are nothing but a control freak. I'm with Isabelle. Nobody ain't messin' with her while she's with me. You haven't even been around her that much. How do you even understand how she feels anymore?"

Rebecca couldn't help herself but be sarcastic. "Of course. You are absolutely right. How can I possibly not know my own bloody sister? How is it that a moron whose ego is so far up his own arse know anything more than me, who has seen more shit than you can ever imagine?"

People eyed them as Rebecca unleashed her fury of words, trying hard not to hit Ryan in front of Isabelle. "If I was a control freak, I wouldn't allow her to date someone like you."

"Someone like me? That's real cute coming from the person who uses her own sister to fill the void for not having a father in her life."

Rebecca had enough, but before she could draw back her fist, she heard a gasp.

"Stop it, Ryan," Isabelle said in a quiet voice.

"Well, it's true. You told me that your father was terrible."

"No … I said he was misunderstood, and Becky wishes he was around more. He's not terrible, but you're mean." And with that, Isabelle walked away from Ryan and joined Rebecca and Alvin.

"I'm sorry, Issy. I didn't mean it like that," Ryan said, panicking. He looked ridiculous trying to beg to her.

"You meant it to hurt my sister's feelings. I love Becky, and I won't tolerate that. I trusted you when I told you about that, and you took advantage of that trust."

"But—"

"I think she's made up her mind, so fuck off."

Ryan's eyes dilated, and his face lost its color. He could've had steam coming from his nostrils as he charged toward the Warren sisters. Rebecca was ready to fight him, but she didn't get the chance. Alvin stood in front of them and *pushed* Ryan back. He crashed to the ground.

"I'm sorry for not telling you where I was going," Isabelle said to Rebecca.

"You shouldn't be sorry!" Ryan yelled as he struggled to stand.

"I agree," Rebecca said. "Issy, you don't need to apologize, but somebody else is about to be sorry if they don't leave us alone."

Alvin approached Ryan, who didn't try anything this time. Instead, he turned and walked away, leaving Rebecca and Isabelle in a hug.

Isabelle joined Rebecca and Alvin on their date, which Rebecca didn't mind at all; although she was worried it might ruin it for Alvin, but he seemed to be perfectly happy with it. Unfortunately, they didn't get to watch the action movie they had planned to see. They let Isabelle pick the movie, since her date was ruined. Now they were stuck watching a film for little kids. Rebecca was okay with it, and Alvin seemed just a bit bothered by it, but the two of them sat behind Isabelle and held hands and cuddled.

They eventually fell asleep on each other, and Isabelle had to wake them. She asked them if they saw certain parts of the film, and both would nod yes and agree with whatever it was she said.

On their walk back to campus, getting past the damaged part of the fence, Rebecca and Alvin slowed their pace, letting Isabelle get ahead a bit.

"Why is it that when we are together, crazy things end up happening?" Alvin asked.

"The arrow, the fire, and now Ryan." Rebecca counted on her fingers.

"Well, at least this time it ended on a good note." He reached for Rebecca's hand and held onto it. "I had a great time with you tonight. Thank you for coming."

"I had a good time too." Rebecca looked at Alvin and noticed his blue eyes shimmering in the moonlight, like waves dancing on the ocean surface.

Their tracks stopped immediately, and they turned to each other as their gazes fixed upon their faces. Rebecca closed her eyes as their lips closed in on one another.

A scream echoed through the woods. She pulled away from Alvin fast who looked stunned. Rebecca searched around for a sign of Isabelle, but she was nowhere to be found. Rebecca ran to where they would have walked if they had kept going.

"Help!" another cry bellowed.

Rebecca heard it from her left side. Without a second thought, she dove into the thicket of bushes and trees. Through briars, leaves, and low-hanging branches, Rebecca raced for the sound of her sister. She looked back only once to see if Alvin was coming, but she was sure that if he was, she was too far ahead. She didn't stop for him. She had to find Isabelle.

Rebecca emerged from the bushes into a clearing. In front of her was Isabelle, gagged and tied up by none other than Annabelle Alexandria. Rebecca dashed forward but stopped immediately as Annabelle put a knife to Isabelle's throat.

"Come any closer and she's dead."

"Let her go!" Rebecca knew Annabelle wouldn't obey, but Rebecca was desperate to try anything. She looked around and realized Annabelle had been camping in the clearing. She had a set of swords, a bow and a quill of arrows, and other tools.

"Stand down, child, and take your place at the sword of your king, Mathias Burgess."

"You won't kill her. You told me that before you killed Blake."

Annabelle grinned. "Hard to forget those small details when something so traumatic happens, isn't it? True, I cannot kill your sister, but I can kill you."

"You won't have a chance." Rebecca gritted her teeth and was about to run at her foe, but before she could act, Alvin jumped from behind and tackled Annabelle to the ground, sending the weapons and tools crashing everywhere. Rebecca took her opportunity and went straight for Isabelle and retrieved the school knife from her back pocket and cut the ropes.

Alvin yelled, and Rebecca saw that his arm had a gushing wound; Annabelle had freed herself from him. As Rebecca turned to Annabelle, Isabelle ran to Alvin and used her gag cloth to try to stop the bleeding.

Annabelle and Rebecca both grabbed a sword from the ground, and it was just like their battle at the airport. Their blades clashed back and forth as they reflected the moonlight, but it wasn't anything like Alvin's eyes. The little flashes ignited when Annabelle would almost decapitate Rebecca.

But Rebecca channeled her magic, and, with a force, it shattered Annabelle's blade—an idea she thought of from Vanessa. She stood in shock and looked at the damage then to Rebecca, who was also amazed at what she did.

"No …" she muttered. "That's impossible. You can't have learned that. You're not allowed to!"

Rebecca swung her sword, and Annabelle dove out of the way. She scrambled to grab her bow and quill, and it felt like the arrows never stopped coming. Annabelle hammed an arrow every second at Rebecca as she ducked between trees. There was no doubt she was a good archer, but Rebecca had another idea.

She stepped from behind the tree and raised her hand. The arrows slowed down and nearly halted in mid-air.

Annabelle kept stringing more arrows, and each one would get caught in the force field. She only stared in shock when she fired her last one.

Rebecca waved her hand around, redirected the arrows toward Annabelle then gave them all a *push*. Almost like lightning, they zipped back toward her. One of them nicked her wrist, causing her to drop the bow. She looked up with anger and frustration.

"This isn't fair!" she shouted then bolted into the trees.

Rebecca chased after her, picking up her sword along the way.

"Wait, Becca!" Alvin called out.

"Watch over Issy!" she said just before she disappeared into the woods. She had to stop Annabelle once and for all.

Through more woods she dashed before she came upon another clearing. This one featured a small pond with a large rock beside it. Rebecca looked around, thinking she couldn't have lost Annabelle that quick.

Sure enough, Annabelle appeared from behind the rock, attempting to jump onto Rebecca with her knife drawn. She was pinned down, but not for long, as Rebecca pushed Annabelle away. Her body collided with the rock hard, and she didn't get up, but Rebecca knew she was still alive.

Rebecca stood and she brushed her hair out of her view. She looked at her hand and saw blood. She touched just below her left eye and felt a deep cut.

"As if I didn't have enough scars from you," Rebecca said as she looked down at Annabelle. She approached her and raised her sword to the woman's chest.

"Go ahead and kill me then, if that's what you want. Do you think it'll make you feel better about losing Blake? I'll give you a bit of advice. It doesn't change anything but who you are."

Rebecca lowered her blade. She wanted to do it so badly. She wanted to see Annabelle dead, but she couldn't. She wouldn't.

Annabelle grinned. "Weak. You won't be able to defend your sister when King Mathias comes for— aghhh!"

Rebecca pierced the blade tip into Annabelle's chest. She used all her raw and magical strength to push deep into the woman's body. She made it so deep that the blade exited the other side and stuck into the ground.

Rebecca screamed at Annabelle. She took the woman's life, and it surprised both of them. She stepped back and surveyed what she had done.

Annabelle's arms were eagle-spread, and her mouth was open. A puddle of blood formed and spilled into the pond.

Rebecca caught her breath after a few minutes. She had just committed murder.

No. She had defended her own life and her sister's and Alvin's. Then she remembered. They were together right now, and sooner or later, they would come looking for her. Rebecca had to get back to them before they found this scene.

Rebecca took one more look at the body, turned on her heels and ran for it.

Chapter 18

The world felt so much quieter despite the rustling and crunching sounds of every step Rebecca took. Her thoughts raced about what she had done. She had killed Annabelle. It was over, at least for now. But Rebecca could never tell anyone what she had done. Not even Morgan or Andrew or even Lucy could know.

When Rebecca returned to the clearing, Alvin and Isabelle were sitting on the ground. Alvin had managed to stop the bleeding on his arm and was comforting Isabelle. As soon as she saw Rebecca arrive, she ran to her. The girls hugged.

"Are you okay?" Rebecca asked. She felt her sister nod against her chest.

"What happened? Where's that woman?" Alvin asked.

"She got away." It was the first thing that came to her mind. "I lost her. We should get away from here before she comes back."

"Agreed," Alvin said. "We should report this to the dean."

"Yes. Let's go. Issy, come on. We're getting away from here."

Isabelle looked at Rebecca, and her eyes widened. "What happened to your eye? Are you okay?"

"It's just a small cut. A thorn got me. I'll be fine."

They hurried toward the main campus. Rebecca agreed about reporting what had happened, because she could never convince them to not say anything. Plus, something Rebecca had learned as a child was whoever told their side of the story first was usually the one to be believed. Rebecca had to tell her story before someone discovered Annabelle's body.

Rebecca clutched Isabelle's hand as they travelled the trail—not just to comfort her sister but Rebecca was afraid of what was coming. Alvin couldn't keep his mouth shut about what had happened. He gave a play by play of the fight between Rebecca and Annabelle. Rebecca nor Isabelle wanted to hear it though. They would have to relive the scene soon enough. Rebecca turned around and told Alvin to stop talking. He was taken aback by the aggressiveness of her tone.

As they reached the central building, they noticed a large presence of adults outside. They didn't waste time with Rebecca leading them inside. About a dozen police officers filled the lobby, and Dean Richardson and Miss Stetson stood by a bench, talking to Melanie Evans.

"Peace be with!" Mr. Richardson exclaimed. "Are you kids all right?"

"Sir, Annabelle Alexandria just attacked us," Rebecca said hesitantly.

"Annabelle?" Melanie asked.

"Yes. She's here."

"We know that," Miss Stetson said. "The police found her body after someone reported hearing a woman screaming."

"She's dead?" Alvin asked.

"A sword had impaled her chest," Melanie said. "We believe someone stabbed her—as in murder."

Alvin regarded Rebecca, who spied Isabelle to avoid any eye contact. She didn't want to look suspicious, but Alvin had seen her pursue Annabelle with her sword. She hoped that Alvin would stay quiet.

Rebecca and Alvin explained what had happened to them. Isabelle didn't say a word. When they reached the part of the story when Rebecca had chased after Annabelle, she simply said that Annabelle had disappeared, without any mention of a sword in Rebecca's hand.

"So, you're saying she just vanished?" Melanie asked.

"Yes."

"Guess you three got lucky," Miss Stetson added.

"We discovered a student near the scene, drunk and talking about a woman in a disturbing manner," Melanie said. "We'll question him first and then speak to you three individually."

"Kids, you all look like you've been through quite a bit," Mr. Richardson said. "Alvin, let one of the medics here check your arm. Rebecca, Isabelle, you two can go to the infirmary."

"Who's the student?" Alvin asked.

"Ryan Bostick."

*****

Rebecca held Isabelle's hand as they travelled to the infirmary. The hallways were quiet with a buzz of lights hitting them every few steps.

"I can't believe Ryan did it," Isabelle said. It was the first thing she'd said since they were in the forest.

"Me too." Rebecca was quite grateful that she got out of the situation so easily, but she wasn't sure how she felt about someone else taking the blame, and credit, for Annabelle's death. At the same time, it couldn't have happened to a better person.

"Should I feel bad that Annabelle is … well, you know …" Isabelle couldn't finish her sentence.

"Try not to think about it."

"But what if I didn't break up with Ryan? Maybe he wouldn't have done it."

"Issy, some people are not who they seem to be. Eventually, they show who they really are."

"I hope you and I never change who we are."

*****

The next day on the morning news, Rebecca and Morgan watched the headline read, MURDER AT CAPITOL STREET: ENGLAND KNIGHT DEAD.

"Last night, law enforcement found Annabelle Alexandria's body in the campus forest of Capitol Street Academy in Washington, DC, stabbed with a sword. Alexandria was the head knight of security for the royal army of England. Back in December, seventeen-year-old and English refugee, Rebecca Warren, had accused Alexandria of murder.

According to the federal police department's press release, they had found Alexandria after someone had notified police of suspicious activities on campus. Police later detained a student nearby, drunk and rambling about a woman he claimed he wanted to be dead.

Currently, there are no other suspects, according to lead investigator, Melanie Evans.

US President Gregory Oppenheimer is calling for a world peace hearing with England's King Mathias Burgess, standing a trial before other leaders for breaking world peace laws. According to Evans, Alexandria was not allowed in the country, and her presence comes across as a potential act of war.

King Mathias has not yet made a statement on the matter at hand.

*****

"This is wild!" Morgan said later when they met with Andrew and Lucy. "I mean, I'm not completely surprised that Ryan did it. He always seemed a little off his rocker. But how in the world did he do it?"

"I don't know, but at least she's gone, and she's not hurting anyone again," Rebecca said.

"I'm glad the world will hold Mathias on trial, more than anything else," Lucy said. "Maybe they'll dethrone him, and we can go home."

"I got the feeling he won't go down that easy," Morgan said. "These things tend to drag out when it comes to politics."

"But one good thing is he can't declare war with anyone," Andrew said. "Oppenheimer has royal blood in him. As long as Mathias is the only person without royal blood as a leader, he can't go to war with any other nation."

Rebecca thought Morgan was right though. Mathias would not be stopped that easily. The world was only safe for now.

"Did you notice the news no longer downplays Blake's death though?" Lucy asked. "Nobody is bashing Rebecca anymore either. Not even Vanessa has said a word about it."

Morgan giggled. "Well, Vanessa knows better."

It was true that nobody in Rebecca's classes seemed to care anymore about the Warrens. It looked as though people were more concerned about Mathias attacking America. By the end of the school year, someone had even started an anti-Mathias club, and the club leader had asked Rebecca to be an honorary member. She had declined, because she didn't want to be part of some silly thing like that.

Miss Stetson seemed to be the only faculty who paid any attention to Rebecca. Their lessons ended a week before exams, and Miss Stetson noted that she was no longer worried about Rebecca handling herself now. After what Alvin had described, she seemed to be a little impressed with Rebecca's actions.

When Melanie talked to Rebecca about her encounter with Annabelle, she appeared to be much more stressed than ever before. She also acted weird with the way she spoke to Rebecca. She had a feeling Melanie knew what Rebecca had done, but she was trying to cover it up. She wondered why Melanie had gone to great lengths to protect her and Isabelle. It just didn't seem right.

As the school year ended, Rebecca searched for Alvin. According to another student, his father had already picked him up after his last exam, so Rebecca moved on to meet with her friends.

Morgan and Andrew were outside of their bus loading their luggage when Rebecca found them. Morgan had confessed that she froze before she was about to ask out Andrew. Rebecca was not surprised, but she smiled when she saw them bickering about how close Morgan was to failing her exams.

"I passed. That's all that matters, right? Cs get degrees."

"But you could do so much better."

"Hey, guys," Rebecca said.

They both stopped and looked at her.

"Becca, will you please tell this nerd to stop and that not everyone is as smart as him?"

Rebecca went to open her mouth, but Andrew cut her off. "How did you do?"

"Er, well, I got through them just fine. If I have to come back next year I can."

"Is it selfish to say I hope you do come back?" Morgan asked. "I'll miss you if you go back to England."

"I'll miss you too. Thank you both for looking out for me this year and being by my side through all this chaos."

"What are friends for?" Andrew asked.

Rebecca pulled them both in for a hug. Morgan and Andrew were the only two Rebecca would miss from this place. But, as she let go and said goodbye to board her own bus, she knew her focus would be on the news to watch Mathias' hearing, and all she wanted to hear was she could safely return home.

She joined Isabelle and Lucy in a seat on their bus. Isabelle was in the middle of drawing something, and Rebecca peered over to look at it, but she pulled it out of sight.

"You have to wait until I'm finished."

A few strokes later, she handed the drawing to Rebecca, and she nearly teared up over it. In the drawing, Rebecca and Isabelle stood surrounded by all their friends. Isabelle and Faith were hugging while Rebecca and Lucy were arms over shoulders. Morgan was flipping back her hair with her vine curled around her finger while Andrew had a book tucked into his arm and was adjusting his glasses. Standing behind them was Blake smiling down on them. He was clean shaven and young looking, like he was in the family portrait.

"This is brilliant, Issy." Rebecca hugged her sister tightly.

Over her shoulder, she looked out the window at the gold C-S-A on Capitol Street Academy's gates. She hoped it would be the last time she ever saw those letters, but not the last she would see the people in the drawing.

The end.

CONTINUE REBECCA'S JOURNEY IN

CAPITOL STREET ACADEMY

~ON THE RUN~

T. RUSSELL PARKER

ABOUT T. RUSSELL PARKER

Russell Parker is from Rockingham, North Carolina. After graduating from Richmond Senior High School in 2015, Russell attended UNC Pembroke studying in Mass Communications-Broadcasting.

Russell continues to live in Rockingham with his three cats, Gizzy, Bandit, and Poppy.

Made in the USA
Middletown, DE
31 July 2023